DEAD IN THE WATER

POLICE SCOTLAND
BOOK 1

ED JAMES

1

Shepherd

The tide was far out to sea, low down in the distance, maybe half a mile away. Some kids were running on the damp sand, leaving footprints that would be washed away soon. The wooden groynes were fully exposed, lying in the evening summer light like the preserved skeleton of a dinosaur. Another one just further along to stop the sand getting sucked out to sea.

Luke Shepherd sat on the wall and stared across the Forth to the Fife coast, the river glistening in the sunshine. He'd worked with someone from Tranent who saw that view from their garden every morning for forty-six years and yet had never thought to visit. Not that Fife could live up to that hype.

He looked back along the promenade at Portobello's faded Victorian glamour, that wasn't so faded these days. An old holiday destination, huge old hotels that went to ruin, but were now on the way back through gentrification. A street food van sold fancy coffees and pastries, even at this late hour. Hell, there was even a bookshop on the high street. And so many artisan food places it was almost like the city centre.

He hadn't been here in a while, maybe ten years. Second-hand cigarette smoke caught on the breeze, mixing with the tang of seaweed. He caught sight of the three idiots bumbling his way, hands deep in fish suppers, the gait of the severely mashed. Now the pubs were open again, it was open season for the idiots to catch up on a year's worth of inside drinking. Even on a day like this.

Scott Cullen was first, sucking down a can of knock-off Lilt and tossing it into the bin. He clicked his finger at Shepherd, pistol pointing at him. 'There he is.'

Shepherd stood up tall and waited. 'Your intel's crap, Scott.'

'How?'

Shepherd nodded inland at the Gothic house. 'The Dalriada shut down last year.'

'Ah, shite.' Cullen stopped dead, but rocked

forward with the exaggerated momentum of the drunk. 'That's a disappointment.' Behind Cullen, Craig Hunter and Malky McKeown stuffed their chip wrappers into the bin, then took turns to finish their cans. Christ, he reeked of booze. 'We could go to the Sheep Heid?'

Shepherd thought it through. On the southern slopes of Arthur's Seat, nestling in the heart of Duddingston, an ancient village, or at least ancient-feeling. Mostly food, with a bit of drinking, but far enough away from anyone who'd know them. Meaning they could talk in safety, but he'd be protected by being out in public. Probably an even better spot than the Dalriada would've been. 'Fine. I'll drive us. Parked up on the High Street.'

'Nice one.' Cullen swung around. 'Change of plan, boys.' He shot off in the direction of Shepherd's car, meeting Hunter at the side street.

Shepherd followed, though he remembered the block of buildings on the left. Someone had lived there, someone involved in that old case. He exhaled and nodded a smile at McKeown. 'You boys been out for a while?'

'Decent sesh, aye.' McKeown burped into his fist. 'Day off today?'

'Something like that.' Shepherd sped up towards his car. 'Pubs in Porty any better these days?'

'Miles better, Luke. Proper hipster lark. Not a patch on the Cheeky Judge, mind.'

Shepherd gave him a bit of side eye as they walked. 'Nice pub that one.'

'The best.'

Cullen and Hunter were already at Shepherd's car. Even hammered, they were fast walkers.

McKeown was running a fingernail between his teeth, then swallowed whatever he'd found. 'See you drive a Tesla, big man.'

'That's right.' The locks plipped as Shepherd neared.

'Mighty expensive on a DS's salary.'

'It's only a Model 3. Practically giving them away. My sister's husband works for Tesla, got me a good deal.'

'Speaking of a good deal.' McKeown stopped to tie his shoelaces. 'I've been in touch with a mutual friend of ours. Brian Bain.'

'How's he doing?'

'He's well. Asking about you.'

Shepherd knew he was up to something. 'Oh?'

McKeown shifted his feet, crouching the other way round, and nodded at the car. 'Told us some things about you, Shepherd. About what you're really up to.'

Shepherd felt his nostrils flare. 'What's that?'

'Well.' McKeown hauled himself up tall, but looked like he was going to totter over. 'Told me about a case back in the day, about how Cullen and Hunter were covering up something.' He dusted off his knees. 'I didn't work it myself, but it might be worth you looking into. Got a big list of people you could have a word with, not all of them still on the force. See if you can get something out of them.'

Shepherd focused on the car. This was something new, some fresh blood to get stuck into. As doubtful as he was of the source, this was a gift horse whose mouth needed a good inspection.

Could he trust Malky McKeown?

Could he trust Brian Bain?

'You're out drinking with them. Why should I trust you?'

'Loose lips sink ships, Luke. And the drunker they get, the looser they get. Seeing what I can get out of them, see what I should pass on to you. What I should keep for my podcast.'

The Secret Rozzer, but Shepherd knew that. 'I'm assuming you've got something?'

'A classic. Think you worked it.'

Shepherd had an inkling of what he was talking about. A case where two plus two equalled four, but not all the time. And not in hindsight. Still, it could be a game. 'You should raise your concerns with Professional Standards and Ethics.'

'I am. Bain said you're still working that beat.'

'Oh, Malky. I'd love an imagination as wild as yours. Not as wild as his, mind.'

'If you're not interested...' He made to walk off.

'I didn't say that.'

'So you're not interested?'

'No, but I like to know who I'm working with. If I can trust them.'

McKeown burped into his fist. 'If it was me, I'd start with Paul Gordon.'

'Elvis? What does he know?'

McKeown shrugged. 'Bain wouldn't say. But he did say Yvonne Flockhart might know a thing or two. Trouble is, she's shacked up with Cullen these days, right?' A thin smile crossed his face. 'And you might want to tie it up with what Bain's been digging up on those pair.'

If Bain was involved, then it might be something juicy. But why get a clown like McKeown to broker it?

Still.

Shepherd got out his phone and held it up. 'Scott? Got a call from Ally. Need to head back into the office. I'll drop you boys where you want.'

2

Becky

Ten years ago
The Friday before Christmas

The tide was in, the water touching the sea defence walls running along the promenade. Becky was standing half the way along, sucking in the strong smell of the sea spray. Brushing her hair back again, before the cold breeze swept it away. The wooden groynes were almost fully submerged. At least, that's what she thought they were called.

Groynes.

Didn't seem right, did it?

Becky didn't know if she could go through with this.

What it all came down to was standing in court, being questioned by lawyers from both sides. Her side, the prosecutors, had her well prepped, or so they said. But maybe what her friends said was true – that they didn't have her best interests at heart. The other side, though... She'd seen it happen on TV, seen them tear apart witnesses on the stand.

And worse, seen them tear apart victims.

Victims like Becky.

And *he* would be there, sitting in the courtroom. Watching her. And his friends would be there, too. All those eyes watching her. Ears listening to her. Someone would maybe wait outside for her. Send her a message she hadn't already ignored.

Her phone bleeped in her pocket, the Taylor Swift tune she'd assigned to him. *The Story of Us.* Felt ironic when she set it, but now? Now... Well.

Becky sat on the bench and hit the green button, her hair catching in a gust of wind. 'Hello?'

'Hey, Becky, it's Luke.'

Shepherd. DS Luke Shepherd.

The rain started up again, splashing her face with a fresh wash. 'Oh, hey.'

'Just checking you're okay?' Said like a question.

Becky owed him the truth. Him of all people. He'd stood by her all this time, helped her through it. Being her rock, the one man she could rely on. 'Not really, no.'

'Want to talk about it?'

Of course she did.

All the nights when she'd actually slept, when she'd woken up with *his* face in her dreams. Her nightmares. A distant memory, maybe, but a vivid one.

And she never wanted to talk about it. Definitely not in front of all those evil faces.

She clutched the phone tighter. 'Not really.'

'Okay, well I'm here for you, okay?' Luke paused. No sounds on the line, so maybe he was in an office. 'Why don't you tell me what's going on?'

'Tough night, you know? Barely slept.'

'Happens a lot, Becky. Believe me. Even tough old cops like me get jitters before we stand up in court. I'll see you there, aye?'

'Aye.'

'Are you sure I can't pick you up?'

'I'm fine. Got my bus pass.'

Another pause, longer this time. 'If you're sure?'

'I'm sure. Thanks for offering, though. Means a lot.'

'Right, well, I'll see you in the cafe down the road, okay?'

'Okay.' Becky hit the end call button and the weight of it all crushed down on her like someone tipping sand on her. Bucket after bucket. Felt like she was drowning in the stuff.

On the thin strip of sand ahead of her, a man threw a ball for his dog, which ignored it and the ball rolled right into the sea. The dog looked at the owner with a frown and a tilted head, then waded into the water and gripped the bobbing ball in its mouth before doggy-paddling back and dropping it at its owner's feet.

Hell, that's how she felt. Shepherd was the owner, her the dog. Maybe she was the ball.

Was she doing the right thing?

Was there even a right thing to do?

Of course there was.

She needed to do this. If they could put *him* away, he'd not be able to do it again to any other women. And maybe she'd feel okay. Maybe she'd sleep again.

Maybe.

But it had to be worth the shot.

Becky pushed up to standing and dusted sand off her trouser legs. No skirt. Luke's advice. Something like victim shaming was horrible, but judges and juries still did it. And she wasn't used to trousers. Jeans, leggings, tracky bottoms, sure. Heels, though, clicking off the tarmac as she walked up to the High Street, taking Bath Street, that long curve up to the crossroads. Jim's flat was two doors up, but he was out, working the early shift in the Deb.

Seeing his stairwell door made her shiver.

Jim had offered to take the day off to support her. Drive her up to the court, sit with her. But no. She told him not to be so daft, to save up his holidays for their break after Christmas.

She nibbled her thumbnail as she walked. Truth was, she wanted him there. Needed him. Holding her hand. Telling her it was going to be okay, whatever happened.

A car slowed behind her and she could hear the window winding down. 'Alright, doll?'

Using that word, it could've been anyone.

But it wasn't, was it?

Becky looked around at the car. Kenny Falconer was behind the wheel of his souped-up Audi. An old thing tinted matt black, which seemed to suck in all the light, not that there was much on a day like this.

Becky sped up, her heels clicking faster even though it was pouring down now.

The car revved its engine, overtaking her and stopping up ahead by the bingo hall. The passenger door opened and a big goon got out onto the road, then stepped around the damp pavement.

Becky couldn't get past him.

The Co-op car park was just beyond him. She could sneak in there, use the lane at the side, then get around to the police station. Maybe? And she could phone

Shepherd, tell him she needed that lift after all. Tell her that Kenny was putting frighteners on her, just like Luke said he might.

Becky got her phone out of her bag. 999 was only for emergencies, right? Was this one?

The big lump snatched it out of her hand. 'Fancy thing, this. One of them newfangled Apple iPhones. Cost a pretty penny.'

Becky knew not to give this creep any satisfaction, so she just gave him that grin. Her favourite one to use on drunks in the bar. 'Give it back.'

'Deano, let her have it.' Kenny was out of the car now. Behind her. She could feel his breath on her neck. Maybe he wasn't that close, but she could *feel* it.

But Deano didn't return it. He pocketed it instead and folded his bulky arms across his big chest.

Nobody was around. Nobody to step in. The rain thundered down now, soaking Becky and this Deano guy, his black T-shirt turning the same tone as the car. He seemed to grow in size, like he was soaking up the rain. Even though Becky was faster than him, heels plus rain put her at a disadvantage.

'Sorry, Becks. Deano's got a mind of his own, eh?' Kenny clapped her arm and it was like she'd been electrocuted.

She reached out to slap him.

Kenny grabbed her wrist. 'Becks, Becks, Becks.

Come on, doll. I've been very patient with you. Mr Vardy here is a mate of mine and he's not impressed by your attitude, are you Deano?'

'Not at all, Kegsy. Not in the slightest.'

'Give me my phone.'

Kenny's voice was in her ear. 'I would, but you're not going to need it, are you?' He was closer now and she could definitely feel his breath on her neck. 'Let's have us a wee chat out of the rain, shall we?'

'Look, I've got somewhere to be.'

'Becky, we know where you're going.' Kenny pressed something into her back. Something hard and sharp. 'Court, where you're going to tells lies about one of our pals. Thing is, we need you to not do that. I've tried being nice, Becks, really I have, but you haven't listened, have you?'

If she just co-operated, then maybe it'd be over soon. But if she struggled? Made a noise? She could see the menace in Deano's eyes. And as for Kenny? She *knew*.

But this was her one chance, wasn't it?

'Kenny, you can't stop me from doing this. I need to.'

'It was a simple misunderstanding.' Kenny pressed the object against her. A sharp blade pierced her leather jacket and jabbed into her back. 'Now, how about you spend some time here with Deano?' He opened the door and pushed her into the car.

3

Cullen

Mid-morning and the station was as noisy as the worst circle of Hell, or at least Acting Detective Constable Scott Cullen's idea of it. The Incident Room was dark. No natural light, no windows, just the smell of thirty sweating bodies toiling away at a case that was already dead in the water.

And the shared secretary with the shrill voice that could cut through diamond, let alone the din of bored cops. *'Good morning, Lothian and Borders. How can I help?'*

Cullen tried to drown it out, tried to focus on the spreadsheet in front of him, but it was a constant distraction. Not that he could justify wearing headphones while he worked.

'Good morning, Lothian and Borders. How can I help?'

FOCUS.

Cullen's screen showed a list of cars the ANPR system had caught at various steps along the City Bypass, coming on and going off. Five days' worth and he had way too many hits for the stretch they were interested in at the time they were interested in. Five in the morning should've been dead, but no. Half of Edinburgh was birling around the Bypass. Each hit was a visit, a chat, maybe some lies, but probably nothing that would help their case any.

'Just putting you through now.' Pause. *'Good morning, Lothian and Borders. How can I help?'*

Cullen sat back and slurped coffee from his stained mug, just the right side of warm. 'Complete waste of time, isn't it?'

DC Craig Hunter huddled into the desk next to him, knees wedged under the wood. Six foot four and big with it. Short-sleeved shirt to show off his arms, but it made him look less a cop and more like a MacDonald's manager. 'Only thing you love more than yourself is moaning.' Then that cheeky grin to show it wasn't meant maliciously. The strip lights caught his scalp through his shaved hair, just a couple of millimetres of stubble and freshly mowed, though he'd missed a patch on the side.

'Craig, Craig, Craig.' Cullen sat back, feeling that prickle of heat he got from pushing a confrontation too far. 'I know you've got me doing this because you struggle to switch on your computer, let alone run the data from the ANPR, but—'

'Seriously, Scott.' Hunter slid his hand across his head. 'It's called "Division of Labour". I've been doing this job years now. You're my Acting DC. You learn from me. Got it?'

Cullen paused, then gave a cheeky grin back. 'How about you show me how to work this spreadsheet, then?'

Hunter looked at Cullen's screen, then sniffed. 'Because that way you won't learn anything. And shite rolls downhill.'

'See, if you looked at it, you could've spotted that I've already got twenty-six hits before I've added in the—'

'Twenty-six?' Hunter rolled his chair closer. 'How?'

'I know.' Cullen tapped the screen. 'Twenty-six cars. Meaning twenty-six owners we need to speak to.'

'Great.' Hunter let his head bounce off his desk. 'People just love speaking to cops the week before Christmas.'

'Not that they ever do.' Cullen finished his coffee,

now the wrong side of warm, and looked around the office. Maybe another cup would help? That tingle he got from too much caffeine, deep in his guts, but this was boring work and he needed to concentrate.

DI Ally Davenport stepped out of his office, the open door letting in some natural light and giving a brief glimpse of the view over to Arthur's Seat, the muscular hill a short walk from the station. Tall as all old-school coppers should be, his thinning hair greased back like a mobster from a film. Black suit, black tie, as though he was heading to a funeral. And chewing gum, the smacking of his lips the only sound that Cullen could hear louder than his secretary's voice. He pointed at someone near Cullen and beckoned them over, then slid back into his office.

Across the desk from Cullen, DS Luke Shepherd hauled himself to his feet like a ten ton truck getting over a railway bridge. As tall as Hunter, but his bear-like build was natural bulk rather than a skinny bugger who spent too long in the gym. Just had to look at a cheeseburger to put on a stone. 'And here we go.' A mutter, probably didn't even know he was saying it out loud. Shepherd slouched off over to the office, tugging at the jacket flapping behind him, the off-the-peg suit not exactly tailored to his mass. Probably lucky to get one in his size in Tesco's Value range.

Cullen leaned in to Hunter. 'What's that about?'

'Probably Davenport looking for an arse to kick when this case goes further south than it's already heading.'

Cullen nodded but, really, he didn't see it was that bad. 'You don't think these number plates will—?'

Hunter laughed. 'Scott, you've got a lot to learn.' He rasped the stubble on his head. 'If those plates had any danger of leading anywhere other than a wild goose chase, Shepherd'd be doing it himself. Or he'd have given it to Yvonne. It's busy work, Scott, hence him giving it to me, knowing I'd get *you* to do it. It's just making sure it looks like Lothian and Borders police have done the job. End of.'

Cullen followed his logic to its natural conclusion. A defeated sigh. 'Right.'

'Good morning, Lothian and Borders. How can I help?'

'That sighing's becoming a habit.'

If that was the case, he just needed to knuckle down. Soak up the busy work, get a name for delivering, then get something a bit juicier.

'No time like the present, eh?' Cullen sat forward and filtered the list to include names and addresses.

'I mean, you could just bugger about with this for a few days, wait until we've caught a wrong 'un or they've shunted this down to the cold case lot. A week until Christmas. No doubt some numpty will stab another numpty over one too many at the office party.'

'Craig, I'm off on holiday tomorrow.'

'Shite, I forgot.' Hunter's turn to sigh now. The weight of the realisation that he'd get the joyous task of visiting these people himself, and without an ADC to blame any inadequacies on. He squinted at the screen. 'Shite, shite, shite. This is going to take *days*. You got numbers for them?'

'That's what these are, Craig. Number plates.'

'*Phone* numbers, you arse.'

Cullen felt himself blushing. No amount of time would ever get him ready for this role, would it? 'That's next.'

'Good morning, Lothian and Borders. How can I help?'

Hunter was frowning at him. 'You okay?'

'Aye.'

'Just, you look like you're going to burst into tears.'

Cullen had to blink a few times.

'Scott, I get it. You're new to the team, struggling with the role, whether you'll ever make the grade.' Hunter was smiling. 'I've been there. I know what it's like. But I'll look after you, okay? Make sure you're vaguely competent in a couple of decades. Or if it doesn't work out, it's not for everyone. And there's no shame in being in uniform. Take Finlay Sinclair, for instance. He couldn't cut it in CID, but he's a solid street copper. Takes a great deal of pride in preventing crimes that arseholes like us investigate, eh?'

'I'm fine.'

'Seriously, Scott.' Hunter waved over at a meeting room. 'We can go and have a chat if—'

'I'm *fine*.' Cullen laughed, but he felt sick. And like he needed to cry. Christ! He nodded over to Davenport's office. 'But what do you think's going on in there?'

'Probably got a call in for some resource to go to the Jambo's protest today. Bunch of arseholes.'

'Says a Hibee.'

'Don't knock the Hibs, Scott. And you're a sheepshagger, right?'

'For my sins, aye. Where I grew up, you chose either of the Dundee teams or the Dons.'

'So why Aberdeen? Why not Celtic or Rangers?'

'Come on, Craig. Really?'

Hunter laughed. 'Fair enough.'

Cullen leaned forward though, swallowing hard. 'Think Davenport's asking Shepherd about me?'

'Why would he?'

'Well, my tenure's up in a couple of months. Then I'll be back to uniform.'

'My worst nightmare.' Hunter blew air up his face. 'Probably take a header off the Forth Road Bridge if I got shunted back. Like that lad in Forensics last week.'

'Exactly.'

'Like I say, Scott, I'll look after you.'

'Good morning, Lothian and Borders. How can I help?'

Cullen stared at the rows of data on the screen, trying to figure out how Hunter was going to actually help him.

The office door swung open and Shepherd darted over, hands in pockets, mouth hanging open. He stopped by their desk and snorted. 'What's going on?'

'We're talking about Hearts and—'

'Lads, if you're talking about football when you should be working, then—'

'*Sarge.*' Hunter held up his hand to cut him off. 'I was going to say, and their fans protesting at Tynecastle at lunchtime.'

'Aye, bollocks you are.' Every so often, Cullen would catch snatches of Shepherd's Borders accent, especially the long drawn out "aye", more like an "oyyy".

'Seriously.' Hunter sat back, head resting on his hands. 'And we were devising a strategy to speak to all these number plates Scott's found in the case. Twenty-six of them.'

'Christ on a bike. I expected three, maybe four.' Shepherd shot his gaze between them. 'Right, well, you're thick as thieves you two.' He raised a finger. 'Make sure you behave yourselves at the Christmas party tonight, aye?'

Hunter folded his arms. 'Why are you giving us that message?' He nodded over to the office. 'Ally think we're trouble?'

'Asked me to mention it to everyone, but you two were mentioned explicitly.'

Hunter looked away. 'Not even sure we should be having a big piss-up in the middle of a murder inquiry.'

'I get that, Craig, but it's for morale. And it's a Friday night. Don't make us look bad, eh?'

Cullen held up his hand. 'We barely drink, Luke. We'll be fine.'

'Aye, like hell you don't.' Shepherd cleared his throat and looked back to Davenport's office. 'Anyway, I need you pair to come with. We've got to follow up on a no-show at a court appearance.'

4

Hunter

Portobello beach bathed in the winter sunshine, a million miles from the kind of dusty hellholes DC Craig Hunter had spent so many years in. Way too many years. The promenade was busy; mums with prams, a horde of young school kids going to the swimming baths. Escaping Porty, just to end up back here. Great.

Shepherd hammered on the door again. 'Bloody, bloody hell. She's run off, hasn't she?'

Hunter looked round. 'Thought Ally spoke to her?'

'*I* did.' Shepherd sighed. 'She said she was on her way. Trouble is, a rape victim has to stand up in court to face her attacker. Odds are stacked against them. And our current system means we have to do everything in CID. Murders, robberies, assaults, rapes. We should shift to the Met's model. Major Investigation Teams. Then it wouldn't be us having to do this sort of thing. Specialists.'

Hunter could see a future for himself in that world. Interrogate the raping bastards, bring them to justice. Support the victims, help them through to convictions. 'Sounds like you've got inside information, Sarge.'

'Wish I did, Craig.'

Cullen came from down the lane, shaking his head. 'No sign of anyone in there. Lights are off, no telly or music playing either.'

Shepherd grinned at him. 'This will be good practice for you when you get back to uniform in a few months.'

Cullen shot him a glare, mouth hanging open.

'Just messing, Scott.'

Cullen frowned. 'So I've got a tenure?'

'Not my place to say. I am sure Davenport will be in touch before the New Year, though. You know most of these acting gigs are for a year. And if you aren't being picked up, then first of January is a great time to return to the street.' Shepherd hammered the door harder and shifted his pattern. 'Miss Crawford? It's the police.' But his slumping shoulders showed he'd given up.

Hunter leaned against the sandstone, arms folded. 'Any ideas, Sarge?'

'She works at this bookshop in town mornings. Pub in the evenings.' Shepherd frowned off into the distance. 'But I think she's been seeing a laddie who works there. Think he lives along the promenade, just at the start of Bath Street. He sat in on some of the interviews with her.'

Hunter set off. 'Where I grew up.'

Shepherd followed, but was out of breath within a few paces. Getting his bulk to shift was clearly a struggle.

Cullen was walking between them. 'My running route, this.' When he could be arsed. Lazy sod talked a good game, but couldn't walk the walk. Or jog the jog. Wouldn't let Hunter take him to the gym either. He pointed up towards the High Street. 'Live just up there, Sarge.'

Shepherd glanced to the side. 'We'll sort out your tenure, Scott. But it might take a while. Might go down to the wire.'

Hunter looked back again. Seemed to have hit Cullen in the gut like a sucker punch.

'Okay.' But he wasn't. Not at all. Almost a year working with someone, going through what they'd gone through and you knew how they reacted to most situations. And Cullen was toiling with the uncertainty.

Welcome to CID.

The tide was slipping back out, but still a way to go until it was at its lowest. Some days you could get half a mile out to sea. Some days Hunter wished he could stay out there. Out to sea, some idiot was in a speedboat, tearing up the deep blue.

Hunter closed on the swimming baths, with the kids queuing up in pairs, hand in hand. The last bench on the wide open area was occupied. And Hunter stopped dead.

Happy Jack sat on the bench, nodding his head in time to some inaudible soundtrack, mouthing words only he could hear. He was skinny, but his Santa Claus beard made him look older and heavier than his years. And he seemed to have cleared any surplus the British army had, and was wearing it all.

A memory flickered in Hunter's brain. The darkness at the edge of his eyesight. The stars in the middle. The smell of dusty desert heat. The taste of gun oil. The feel of a machine gun in his hands.

Hunter held the door open. 'Sarge?'

Braithwaite stood there, eyes narrowing as he held up an open hand. 'Not sure about this, Craig. Might be a trap.'

Footsteps rattled next to him. 'What's up, Craig?' Cullen, resting a hand on his arm. 'You okay?'

No.

No he wasn't.

Every time Hunter had seen him since those days, twice in uniform and once as a detective, Happy Jack had two wives with him. His words, claiming some ownership of another two homeless lives. But now he'd doubled the ranks, with two women either side of him, hugging into him. Another two stood on the tidal defence wall in front, dancing in ultra-slow motion. More like tai chi, than a drugged-up rave or that weird thing Hunter had seen during the summer's Festival, where a group wearing headphones danced down the Royal Mile in eerie silent synchronicity. But they moved like they were all hearing the same beat.

Aye, Happy Jack and his wives were away with the fairies. No sign of any bottles of cider or cheap vodka. Meaning drugs.

Just great.

Shepherd muscled Hunter out of the way, one of the few men who could, and stood between Jack and the wives on the sea wall. 'Shite.' He lurched forward and grabbed hold of the woman to Jack's left.

Hunter shot over and stopped dead. The woman was convulsing, plumes of white foam pouring out of her mouth.

The wife on the other side started doing the same.

And Happy Jack didn't care, just kept singing without sound.

Cullen got out his crappy Nokia and held down the

speed dial. 'Control, this is ADC Scott Cullen on the Promenade at Portobello, just outside the Dalriada pub. Need a couple of ambulances. Possible drug overdoses, two adult females.'

And Hunter had to keep them alive for that long.

Great. Just bloody perfect.

'Okay. I'll hold, but I need them urgently. Aye, thanks.'

Shepherd held one of them, staring into the wife's eyes, rolling back in her head.

Braithwaite stopped dead, eyes shut. The women all lay on a massive bed. Ten of them. Only one of them breathing, but faint and shallow.

Hunter stepped closer to her, but Braithwaite nudged him back. 'It's too late, Craig.'

'It's not too late, Jon, we can—'

Someone grabbed Hunter's shoulders and shook him.

He jerked forward and clattered his fist into his sternum. Cullen tumbled over the low wall and disappeared.

What the hell? Where was he? He managed to focus on Cullen. 'Scott?'

Cullen popped his head up and started dusting himself off. Sand everywhere, over his hair, his suit, his trousers. He leaned down to pick up his phone, frowning at Hunter like he'd lost all trust in him.

'Hello? I'm still here.' He pointed at the bench behind Hunter 'Get hold of Jack!'

Hunter swung around. Jack was on his feet now, looking like he was going walkabout. Hunter jerked forward and grabbed Jack's wrists, and pushed him back on the bench. The big man started wriggling like a small child, but with the power of an ex-soldier.

Still, Hunter was a lot stronger than him, and was younger and fitter, and without the malnutrition of a life on the streets. And wasn't smacked out of his skull.

'Craig, the ambulances have been dispatched. They'll be ten minutes.'

'How long would it take you to drive there?'

5

Cullen

The reason for the ambulances taking forty minutes was clear to Cullen when he got close to the King's Road roundabout. A three-car accident, blocking the Harry Lauder Road around Portobello. But he managed to sneak through the tight gap between two maroon buses, and floored it, on the wrong side of the road, and shot off towards Piershill.

Not the fastest route to the hospital, but it was *a* route and he'd get them there in minutes.

'Next left.' Hunter was in the back with Happy Jack's wives.

That back road led up to Arthur's Seat and the park.

Meaning they could get to Danderhall that way, then it was a straight run to the hospital.

'Any idea what they're on?'

'Heroin, probably. But it could be superstrong ecstasy. Hell, it could even be spice.'

'Spice?'

'Christ, Scott, you need to read up. Super-strong cannabis that's eating up Manchester just now. Makes people go nuts.'

'They're foaming at the mouth, though.'

'True. They're barely breathing and I can't feel her pulse. Christ, her tongue shouldn't look like that.'

'Heroin, then.'

'Right.' Hunter was scowling, but his eyes were blank, like he wasn't even in the same car. Made Cullen feel like he was the only one here. And he was supposed to be the one training for the role.

Cullen slowed at the top of the street. A wave of traffic was coming from the lights at the Jewel. Cullen kicked down and blasted out, just managing to get in ahead of the first two cars. There, in and done. A forty zone, but he tore along the road, pushing the needle towards sixty. The lights ahead were clear at least.

'I don't think these two have got long for this world.'

❖

'Here.' Hunter handed Cullen a coffee in a beige plastic cup. 'You did good, kid.'

Cullen took the cup but the last thing he needed was more caffeine, especially not after that drive. His heart was racing. He needed a cocoa, a bath and his bed. Pipe and slippers, trusty hound lying at his feet. But at least the bitter smell took his mind away from the hospital corridor and the disconnected screams. 'Craig, I'm three months older than you.'

'Aye, but you act like you're fifteen.'

'Charming.'

Maybe Hunter had a point, though. Wasn't the first time he'd been accused of being immature.

Cullen took another sip of the coffee and tried to get the shiver out of his system.

Hunter's phone chirped and he checked it. One of those new fancy Apple phones. Posy git. Miles better than Cullen's battered old Nokia. 'It's Shepherd.' He walked off, putting his phone to his ear, slurping coffee. 'Aye, Sarge, we've got them here, though it was like being at Alton Towers the way Cullen was driving.' He disappeared around the corner.

Leaving Cullen on his own.

Something hit him in the chest, made it tighten.

Relief?

Anger?

Stress?

Maybe disgust at the state of Jack's wives.

Maybe empathy at the state of their lives, at whatever traumas had led them to seek solace in Happy Jack's arms and his copious drugs.

'You saved their lives.' Dr Helen Yule was standing in the doorway, leaning against the frame. Fist on her slender hip, glasses catching the bright lights. 'But then your thing is being a hero cop, right?' She rolled her eyes.

Just like *her*. That coquettish smile matched with frosty eyes. Her words encouraging him to do things he shouldn't.

Christ, get a grip!

Cullen put on a mask of a smile and hid behind it. 'Just doing my job, Helen.'

A nurse walked past.

Helen slapped his arm. 'Please use my title when we're on duty, Constable.'

'Okay, *Doctor*.' Cullen had that squirming feeling in his gut. 'How are they?'

'Stabilising. We've administered Narcan to inhibit the effects of the heroin, but now it's just time and respiratory support. As they were frothing at the mouth, we have intubated them. They've aspirated their stomach contents and may have an infection potential. We should see a positive response soon.'

Cullen blew air over his coffee. He couldn't bring himself to look at her. 'Any chance we could—'

Her laugh cut him off. 'No, Scott. No chance.'

'You don't know what I was going to ask.'

'You were going to ask if you could speak to either of them.'

Which wasn't true.

He was going to ask if they could try their date again, but that door was most definitely closed.

Especially when someone doesn't answer the phone to you.

But there was a deeper reason for it all, wasn't there? One he didn't want to face.

'Tell me this isn't because of our—'

'I'm a professional, Scott. Of course it's nothing to do with that.'

'I'm not doubting your professionalism, but part of me feels—'

'Scott, two weeks? And nothing? Seriously?'

'Eh?' Cullen stood up. 'But I've been calling you!'

'Well, my phone hasn't been ringing.'

'Seriously. I tried, sixteen times.'

'Not hard enough.'

That was how she wanted to play it? Fine.

The frothy surface of his coffee was seriously interesting now.

Helen left her perch by the door and walked over to him. Almost as tall as him. 'Scott, we went on a date and we had sex. And you just left me for dead? That's *really* low.'

'I know.' Cullen stood his ground, though. He tasted something acid in his throat. 'And it would be if I'd actually done that.'

'Don't lie to me, Scott.'

'Seriously. I've tried calling you, Helen. Sixteen times, like I say, but if you don't answer, then... And things have been manic at work. We're on this serial rape case and—'

'You honestly expect me to believe any of that?'

It was the truth. Well, part of it. Something stopped him from— 'Karen McFarlane, Debbie Smith, Alison Aitchison. Tell me you don't recognise those names.'

She looked away, eyes shut. 'I know them.'

'Good.' Cullen winced. 'I don't mean good. What's happened to them is terrible. I mean—'

'Scott, a text would've been fine. We could've had a conversation, a dialogue. But you shut me out.'

'I texted you a few times. I called. If anyone's giving anyone the cold shoulder, it's *you*.'

She frowned. 'I don't believe you.'

Cullen got out his phone and found the texts. 'There. See?'

She looked at it. 'Shite.' Then she frowned. 'You absolute idiot. You put in the wrong number.'

'Eh?'

'Mobile numbers start with a seven, Scott. And you're supposed to be the cop.'

'Crap.' Cullen wanted to smash the phone off the floor. 'Bastard thing.'

'It wouldn't have even dialled.'

'This one does. It just went "click brrrr". I thought you'd blocked my number.'

'Oh.'

'Okay, but from your reaction, it feels a hell of a lot like you're saying you want to go on a second date with me?'

She raised her sculpted eyebrows, thin pencil lines. 'Scott, I've spoken to a few nurses here. A lab technician and a paramedic. Word gets around.'

He had no idea what she was talking about. 'About what?'

'My experience is not unique. You shag them, then dump them.'

Right.

There was that one woman. Emma? Erica? She might've been a nurse.

'Look. Aye. Okay. So I've had flings. One-night stands. It's... It's a psychological crutch for me.' He looked at her, made eye contact through her glistening glasses. 'But you're special, Helen.'

She laughed. 'Bullshit.'

'I mean it. You really are. I'm shocked that you can't see it.'

Her scowl softened to an even expression. Maybe the charm offensive was working.

Cullen tried a smile on for size. 'And I swear it's not because you're a Hibs fan, either.'

She tossed her head back.

Bingo.

Cullen felt the butterflies flapping in his stomach, so he widened the smile. 'And I appreciate you asking me if I wanted to go to the Dons match with you. I don't want to mess things up with you, Helen. I texted, yes. I called, yes. But I should've come here, and asked to see you. But I swear, I've been too busy with work, and that's the truth. So busy that I can see why doctors complain so much about long shifts.'

She was grinning now. Maybe a slight twinkle in her eyes. Could just be the lights catching her glasses.

'And I mean it, Helen, you're very different to those nurses, the lab tech, the paramedic and the radiologist.'

'A *radiologist*?'

'That's a joke.' Cullen held up his hands. 'Look, I had a thing with a nurse here, that's true. But I swear the other two... I knocked them back. Kim and Claire, right?'

She paused. Then swallowed. 'Right?'

'They tried it on with me in here, both of them. Same day. No idea what was going on. And I told them both the same thing, I wasn't interested in them. This was after you.'

She stared at him for a few seconds that felt like hours. 'Fine, let's try a second date then.' She held up a finger. 'But I'm picking the place. And you're paying.'

'Sure.'

'Mm.'

'Anyway, how are the wives?'

'The *wives*?'

'It's what Happy Jack calls his lady friends.'

'That's pretty sick.' She led Cullen into an office that looked into the ward. A team of nurses huddled around two beds. 'We've had a few cases like this, but we only get them just at the point of death and then I have to deal with that pathologist. Deeley. The little creep.'

Cullen shrugged. 'Never met him.'

'Well, I'd advise you don't.'

'So, can we speak to them?'

'No.' She sighed. 'Okay, Scott. Here are the rules. Right now we need to work on saving their lives. I mean, your crazy driving did most of that, but usually with cases like this, where there's no fixed abode, we don't stand a chance. Like I say, it's usually a case of finding the corpses, or when paramedics find them alive they're DOA or as near as damn it. These two, they'll live. And there's a fighting chance it'll be without too much long-lasting trauma. But you won't be able to speak to them for a while.'

Someone squelched down the corridor towards them. Hunter, huffing out a breath, staring at Cullen. 'Scott, Luke wants me back at the ranch. Told you to stay here and babysit them.'

'Why? I don't think they'll be going walkabout.'

'Thing is, Luke's found a decent quantity on the other two. And he's worried these two have a condom-full in, ahem, nature's suitcase. Besides, he says Chantal Jain was looking into a series of overdoses. So... you've got to stay.'

And just like that, Cullen's day of actual proper police work reverted back to bloody donkey work. And waiting on two heroin addicts to pass heroin. Or rather, waiting for the doctor to extract it.

'See you around.' Hunter charged off down the corridor.

Helen looked Cullen up and down. 'I need you to leave this with me.'

'You heard him. I'm not going anywhere. You don't think they'll be okay to speak soon?'

'I wouldn't bet my mortgage on it, no.'

'Okay. Thing is, we need to know what they've taken. If we can trace it back to a dealer, then we can either prosecute or at least stop any more overdoses.'

Helen sighed again. 'Let me see if I can accelerate the blood tests. We might be able to match it with other recent samples.'

6

Hunter

Hunter had that deep hunger he only got when he hadn't eaten for a whole day. Which was carelessness more than anything, but it was a common occurrence when you were a cop doing intermittent fasting like those Hollywood actors did to get shredded. Bloody difficult feeling like your body was eating your bodymass when you were stuck in a tiny interview room with Luke Shepherd and Happy Jack.

Hard to decide who smelled worse.

Shepherd's cologne had a whiff of wet dog about it. Probably some fancy fragrance he'd picked up at an airport, supposed to smell all rugged. Bear Man by Chanel.

And no lawyer, just Jack and the strange soft marshmallow smell of heroin mixed with a rancid reek, like he'd been sleeping in a bin. The soft grin and soft focus of a smackhead. His thick beard contained the stains of a good few meals, but few good ones. Sandwiches stolen from Tesco. Greggs sausage rolls dumped in bins.

And Hunter didn't feel hungry anymore.

Still, Hunter knew him, alright. 'Jack.' He locked eyes with him. 'Jack?'

Still nothing, just blissful ignorance.

'Jonathan.'

Shave the beard, wash the months of dirt off, trim the hair, and there he was. Staff Sergeant Jonathan Stephen Braithwaite, as was, hidden behind Happy Jack's cheery exterior.

Dishonourable Discharge in 2006 for an incident in Baghdad. One Hunter had heard so many rumours about that he doubted it all.

Jack was frowning at Hunter, but it was like Braithwaite was doing it. 'Corporal Hunter.' The frown deepened. 'Can't remember your first name, though.'

'It's Craig. You remember me, Jonathan?'

Jack nodded, eyes screwed shut. 'Aye. Corporal Craig.... Can't remember your surname.'

'Hunter.'

'Oh. Aye. How's Terry doing?'

'He's not so good. Not so good at all.'

'Shame. Good laugh, him.'

'How you doing, Jonathan?'

'Don't call me that.'

'Why not?'

'People call me Jack these days, Craig.'

'Happy Jack.'

Jack bared his lips. '*Never* that.'

'Sorry. How you doing, though?'

'Fine and dandy.'

'From all that heroin, aye?'

Jack shrugged. 'Sure you should be interviewing a junkie while he's all hopped up?'

'Aside from the fact you've been cleared for interview by the station's duty doctor, I don't think there's a time when you're not "hopped up".'

'Fair comment.' Jack looked around the room. 'All of you. You're all spying on me, watching everything I do!'

Hunter knew this wasn't going to be easy, but the man's brain had rotted way past the point of rationality. 'Nobody's spying on you, Jack.'

'Aye, you are.' He stood up and wafted his reek over Hunter again. 'Let me out!'

Hunter just stayed where he was. Counting to ten.

And he looked over at Shepherd, arms folded in that way of his, high across the chest. Aye, he wasn't exactly pleased with this.

Hunter motioned with his hand, trying to calm him. 'Jack, take your seat again, please.'

'You can't coop me up in here. I'm a free man!'

'Jack, you might be a free man, aye, but you need to help us.'

'Nonsense!' Jack thumped back in his chair. 'You're going to stick microchips in us, so you can track us.'

Bugger it. 'How?'

'GPS.'

'And what's powering these chips?'

'Us. Our energy.'

'Sounds like amazing technology.'

'I'm saying nowt. Don't want the Chinese to overhear this.'

'The Chinese?'

Jack slid an imaginary zip shut along his lips.

'Why do people want to track you?'

'Because we *know*.'

'You know, do you? Know what?'

Jack laughed. 'I'm not falling for that trick. You'll need to get it from my brain once you've killed me.'

'Come on, Jack. We're old friends. Served in the same regiment. Remember?'

'Aye, just at the start of your service.'

'I was a private, aye. But you helped me get to corporal. You were one of the good guys.'

'I had a lot of time for you, Craig.'

'What happened to you, Jack?'

'Saying nothing.'

'See, I heard that you got chucked out. Next thing I know, a few years later and I'm a cop walking the beat in Portobello. And there you are, Jack. Living on the beach in a tent. With two women.'

'And you've got them, haven't you? Mary and Katie. Stuck microchips in them! Programmed them to divulge all my secrets!'

'They're in rehab, Jack. Mary's living with her parents again. It's been tough for her, after that car accident, but she's getting through the trauma.'

Jack just growled.

'And after that, we kept on bumping into each other when I was in uniform, didn't we? Until I got this job.' Hunter tugged at his suit, way too tight but he had three-hundred-kilo deadlifts four times a week to thank for that bulk. Hundreds of burpees a day. And a ridiculous diet. 'What happened to you? What made you give up your life to do this?'

'Sure you want to know?'

'Of course I do, Jack. I've got my own scars.' Hunter

felt something wash over him again. Stars pricked his vision. And worse — he was running down a hill, somewhere hot and dusty, gunshots ringing out.

One.

Two.

Three.

He knew exactly where it was.

Four.

Five.

Six.

He didn't want to think about what happened next.

Seven.

Eight.

He *never* wanted to think about that time. Never again.

Nine.

Ten.

And he was back in the room.

Jack's infection smell.

Shepherd's cologne.

His own deodorant. The taste of instant coffee still on his lips.

Aye, he didn't want to go back there.

Hunter had a full-on flashback when he'd seen Jack earlier on the promenade. Almost killed Cullen when he snapped him back to reality. He needed to tread carefully here. 'Jack, what happened to you?'

'Like you care, you creepy son of a bitch.'

Hunter leaned forward on his elbows. 'I care a great deal, Jack. Try me.'

Spittle flew from Jack's mouth. 'You really want to know about my life?'

'Aye, Jack. Everything.'

'Don't believe you.'

'Jonathan Braithwaite was a good guy. What happened to him?'

'That *NAME*.' Jack shut his eyes, clamping them tight. 'In Iraq, would be your first tour. Young grunt, skin and bone weren't you? Well, mind when we had a run out to the desert on foot?'

Hunter could taste the dry heat of the air. 'Aye, I remember.'

'Thing was, we were out there, the three of us. You, me, Terry and that boy Mowat. We were doing a recce, right? Scout the land from up on that hill.'

Hunter could see the rise now, that smooth curve. He could taste the sand in the air, feel the heat on his skin, the sweat on his forehead. Hear the muffled screaming.

'Mind we could hear this sound? All of us searching for it.' Jack leaned forward and breathed petrol over them. 'But that wee daft sod, young Mowat, he tripped on this thing. Terry clocked it first. A handle. It wasn't a hill. It was a doorway. And we went down, Craig, didn't we?'

Hunter felt the warm metal of the ladder in his hands, even in this cold room. Like he was back there. No, he *was* back there. He could taste the incense hanging in the air before he smelled it.

'It was this warlord's personal harem, wasn't it? He had these lassies down there. Twenty, thirty. And they were really suffering at this boy's hands. Strapped down on big, big beds, while his mates... Sickening, it was. Absolutely sickening.'

Hunter could hear the grunts, the moans, the muffled screams. The sound that got them searching, that lured them inside. The shock as Terry shot two of the guards with his pistol, both through the head. Bang, bang. Then Hunter and Mowat leaping into action to catch the other two before they could flee, or before Terry shot them. 'I remember it like it was yesterday.'

'Well, Craig, that is what happened to make me leave. Those women. I could see the suffering. We spoke to the lassies, some of them even spoke English, but I have the gift of many languages. They were all from difficult backgrounds across that great nation. But they were all exploited by men who were supposed to look after them. They were all kept in an UNDERGROUND BUNKER WHILE MEN RAPED THEM!' Jack's voice rattled around the room. 'And we took him down, our friendly neighbourhood warlord, didn't we? But he came back as a politician, didn't he?' He snarled. 'Can never keep a bad man down, Craig. And I just wanted to make these women happy.'

'By getting them hooked on smack?'

Jack laughed. 'Craig, my man, you just don't get it. When I meet them, they're already on it. A cop like you, you should know the stats. Homeless women are much more likely to be on hard drugs than men.'

'Okay, but what are you doing for them?'

'I'm getting them good stuff, Craig. Not sharing needles. Not injecting rat poison. Keeping them safe.'

'Thing is, the heroin you've been giving them has resulted in two of them being hospitalised.'

Jack frowned.

'Ah, shite. Why?'

'Overdosing on heroin will tend to do that to someone.'

'You're still lying to me.'

'No, Jack. I'm not. Those four women you were with, though, two of them are in hospital, dying. And the other two are really toiling. Touch and go whether they need to be admitted to hospital as well. And while you might be okay, we can't speak to them.' Hunter sat back, arms folded. He could lie to Jack, see where it got to. Ah, sod it — it's worth it. 'Probably won't get to them before they die.'

'Ah, shite almighty.'

'We need to—'

'You're *lying*.'

'Excuse me?'

'You're lying to me, Craig.'

But the lie was getting him somewhere. He was shocked by it. As hard as it was to openly lie like this, sometimes the ends really did justify the means. 'It's the truth, Jack. We need to know where the heroin comes from. Stop others suffering the same fate.'

Jack stared at him for a few seconds, then shook his head and stared at the wall behind Hunter.

The door opened and Scott Cullen peered in, his face chiselled with designer stubble. He nodded at Hunter, then Shepherd.

Hunter leaned forward. 'Interview suspended.' He hit pause and stood up. 'Be back in a minute, Jack.'

'No worries, son.' Happy Jack was back, banishing Jonathan Braithwaite to history.

Hunter followed Shepherd out of the room, hoping he could bring Jonathan back when he needed to.

Cullen was leaning against the wall, kicking his free foot back to rest on the paint. 'Sorry, chaps, but what he just said, it checks out with what Yule said.'

Hunter smirked at Cullen. 'Yule, aye?'

Cullen shrugged. 'Dr Helen Yule, aye. What of it?'

'Scott, don't tell me you—'

'Shh.' Cullen put a finger to his lips. 'Don't ask, don't tell.' He sniffed. 'Dr Yule reckons both wives are on heroin.' He swallowed. 'They, uh, delivered their packages.'

As gross as it was, Hunter felt some amusement at the thought of Cullen waiting for them to drop their guts. 'Aye?'

'Had to deliver the contents,' Cullen covered his mouth with a fist, 'to the drug squad, who told me to await their input. Told us to speak to a Chantal Jain in the drugs squad about it.'

'Okay.' Shepherd got out his phone. 'I know Chantal. I'll give her a bell. You two get in there and see if you can get the name of a dealer.' He wandered off down the corridor.

Hunter put a hand on the door but didn't open it. 'Thought you were playing hard to get with Helen, Scott?'

Cullen seemed to grimace, but like most things with him, there were whole volumes unspoken in that sigh. 'Hard to when she's looking after your case for you, eh?'

'Suppose so.'

'But I'm not, Craig.' Cullen was looking right at him. 'I've been trying to phone her and she wasn't answering. Turns out I had the wrong number.'

Hunter laughed. 'You daft sod.'

Cullen was scratching his neck now.

Hunter held the door open for him. There was something there, a whole book unspoken. A whole saga. But Hunter didn't know if he was the guy to get it out of him. 'Get things running again, would you?'

'Sure.' Cullen entered the room and started things up again.

Hunter stayed, barely listening, just trying to make sure he wasn't back in that roasting metal container in the desert.

The smells of sweat and oil.

The grunting.

The screaming.

The ominous feeling of pain and hatred that seeped deep into the sand.

Hunter shook himself hard and sucked in a deep breath. 'How are they doing, Scott?'

'One's pulling through. The other... Helen's less sure.'

'Okay.' Hunter entered the room again and sat, locking eyes with Jack. A pathetic sight, his wild hair standing up on end. 'Okay, so the update from the hospital is those two women are at death's door, Jonathan.'

Another lie, but close enough to the truth.

Jack snarled. 'Told you not to call me that.'

'Aye, I know you did. And you think Jonathan Braithwaite died when you murdered said warlord-cum-politician. Well, fate isn't so kind to you, Jonathan. You might think you're Happy Jack, but you're also ex-Staff Sergeant Jonathan Braithwaite. And Happy Jack is just as bad, probably worse. You keep saying about how you want these women to be happy, but you're just supplying heroin to them, the drug that slowly kills them. Or quickly in this case. You're keeping them addicted. Keeping them slaves to their traumas, just like back in—'

'SHUT UP!'

Hunter had him rattled now. 'How are you paying for it?'

'None of your business.'

'Thing is, me and Scott here were chasing down a witness who didn't show in court today and we saw you and your friends all off your faces. Two of you were overdosing and we had to drive them to the ERI at breakneck speed to save their lives. So you can't tell me it's none of my business, Jonathan.'

'Ignorant bastard.'

'How am I ignorant?'

Jack sat back, shifting his oily gaze between Hunter and Cullen. 'You've no idea, do you?'

'Who is your dealer, Jack?'

'My guy.'

'Who is he?'

'That's it. My guy.'

'Right. Jack, we need his name.'

'Nope.'

'It's better if it comes from you. Tell us where you got the heroin. We'll keep you out of jail. We'll keep the RMP away from you.'

'The RMP?'

'Royal Military Police, Jack.'

'I know what it stands for. Why?'

'Well, for murdering an Afghan politician. We've got you on the record admitting to it. You got off with a dishonourable discharge only because they couldn't get the charges to stick. Now you've confessed. Talk now, and we'll keep quiet.'

'No.'

'That heroin is killing people, Jack.' Hunter leaned forward again. 'Your two wives are at the ERI just now. Don't know their names. Maybe we'll only find out when they die.'

Jack inspected his fingernails, but they were so chewed-down and grubby that he didn't bite them. 'Fine. He works at the gym.'

'The gym?'

'Rock Hard Gym.'

'And his name?'

'The Viper.'

Hunter sat back with a Cullen-sized sigh. 'Stop it,

Jack, or I swear to God, you're spending the night in the cells.'

'Craig, mate. The boy's called the Viper. That's all I have. No idea what his real name is. Seriously. I don't lie.'

Show me a junkie who doesn't...

7

Cullen

Hiding out in the Observation Suite meant avoiding the constant din of inane chatter from the interview room but, now the interview was over, the speakers were just playing back empty room sound. Well, almost empty. Just Happy Jack scratching himself on the screen. And something in the speakers made it compress and amplify the sound so it was like Cullen's head was inside Happy Jack's pants.

The best thing to do was to distract himself. His finger hovered over the 9 key, ready to tap it twice to get an x after the space. He tapped it and examined the message:

Good seeing you earlier. Sorry I've been such a dickhead. Thanks for the second chance x

Was that kiss too flirty?

Did it need another?

Should it be upper case?

He sat back, thinking it through. Was he doing the right thing? Sparing her feelings? Trying to conquer his past? His own trauma?

Christ. What a mess he was.

And the door opened.

Shite.

He hit send and put his phone away.

But it was just Hunter. 'Scott?'

'Craig.'

He was scowling. 'You texting someone?'

'Just a lead.'

'You want to share it with me?' Hunter held his gaze. 'Or do you want to jump in at the last minute and grab all the glory like in that interview?' He jutted his chin towards the screen.

Happy Jack was not talking to himself, but at least he'd stopped scratching himself so vigorously.

Cullen eased himself out of his chair. 'Chill, mate. Just following orders.'

'Would've been nice to have that info before we started.'

'Would've been—'

Hunter grinned. 'Just winding you up, mate. It's cool.'

Cullen blew air up his face. Definitely wasn't blushing. 'Okay. I get you. Good one.'

'So, all that stuff about the drugs. That's legit?'

'Aye. On the level. But you looked like you already had him on the ropes, Craig.'

'He's a tough one is Happy Jack. Staff Sergeant Jonathan Braithwaite. Half a life spent in the army, then the rest living on the streets like that.'

'Right, right.'

The door opened and Shepherd blundered in. He was all red in the face, but Cullen couldn't figure out from what. 'Lads. You know DC Chantal Jain?'

Cullen shook his head. But his jaw almost dropped.

'Morning, boys.' Jain was of Asian ancestry, Pakistan maybe, and had the ripest local accent. Cullen could almost name the street just off Ferry Road where she'd grown up, that kind of Leith accent that sounded almost soft Glasgow, despite being opposite sides of the country. Her black hair was tied back in a swaying ponytail. And she was gorgeous. Seriously pretty. 'Craig, I know you. Not in the biblical sense, mind.'

Hunter grinned. 'Not yet, anyway.'

Shepherd rolled his eyes. 'Can you two get a room?'

'Oh, Luke, but Craig's already taken, isn't he?'

Hunter shrugged, neither confirming nor denying it.

Cullen would bet his paltry savings on Hunter's girlfriend not being too happy with this. He thrust out a hand. 'DC Scott Cullen.'

Shepherd smiled. '*Acting* DC.'

'Well, ADC Cullen, it's a pleasure to meet you.' Jain shook his hand like a clamp, but she wouldn't look at Cullen, just kept her focus on lover-boy Hunter. First time in a while that'd happened to Cullen. 'Anyway, so you're the wankers who got that drugs lead?'

Hunter laughed. 'The very wankers.'

'Well, then.' She walked right up to him, then sat down in front of him. 'This Happy Jack guy. Is he on the level?'

'He's on several Class A's.' Hunter gave a flash of his eyebrows. 'Whatever he can get his hands on.'

'But it sounds like you broke through his defences?'

Hunter flexed his pectorals just then. Bad boy. 'We served together.'

'Oh, right. I see.' Jain sat back and took out a wad of paperwork. 'And you got intel that someone's dealing heroin from that gym?'

Cullen butted in. 'I had to wait for them to—'

'Aye, aye.' Jain sat back with her BlackBerry in front of her face. 'Well, thanks for your donkey work in ferrying the sample down to us. We've got this fancy new machine that processed the contents of that condom double quick. It's an unusually pure strain. "Afghan tear-up" is the street name.'

Hunter barked out a humourless laugh. 'Don't talk to me about Afghanistan.' He looked away. 'That why you're here?'

'Had a few cases. Managed to cross-check against two deaths three months ago. Same drug, same purity. Thing is, they thought they'd got it all, but now it's back.

Hunter folded his arms, almost popping the sleeves of his shirt. Christ, he was like Arnold Schwarzenegger in his bodybuilding days, posing and flexing for the crowd. 'Part of that was Scott's quick thinking. Got the doc to—'

'Well, I'm still impressed.' Jain unfolded a sheet of paper and smoothed it down on the table between her and Hunter. 'As you know, Craig, me and DI Wilkinson are on secondment to the Drugs Squad. Mostly intel support, but that means there's a lot of stuff I can dig deep into for you.'

Christ, it was like she was in a job interview. If that's the kind of bluff and bluster you needed to get a full tenure as a DC, then Cullen had a *lot* more training to do.

Hunter picked up another chair and sat on it, backwards. Edgy, but in a late eighties kind of way. 'So, what have you found?'

'Well, like the name says, we think it's from Afghanistan. And it's on a tear-up, that's for sure. Upshot is your dafties overdosing are the first survivors of a few here in Edinburgh. Thing is, we thought we'd stopped it. It went all quiet on the western front for a month and we were going to come back to mainstream CID, then Big Luke here calls me up out of the blue.' She stared hard at Hunter again. 'Assuming it is the same stuff, that's bad news.'

Cullen cleared his throat and got the two lovers to break off eye contact. 'Two of the ODs are in intensive care. Dr Yule suspects they're new to the habit as their three associates are okay-ish with that dose.'

'Well, that *is* good news, I suppose.' Jain tapped her nose and pointed at him. 'So the other three amigos are long-haul smackheads with a high tolerance?'

'Pretty much, except it's one amigo and two amigas.'

'Interesting.'

Shepherd clapped his hands together, like a blast of thunder. 'Right, so here's the game plan. DI Davenport's got an appointment with Chantal's boss in drugs this afternoon, down in Fettes. But he wants us to get around this now.'

Hunter smiled. 'Meaning you're in charge?'

'Correct. Chantal and I will go through her old cases, see if there's anything we're missing.' Shepherd leaned back against the door, hands in pockets. 'Craig,

Scott, I need you to go to this gym and work out, see what you can shake loose on this Viper.'

Cullen frowned. 'We're going undercover?'

Shepherd laughed. 'No, Scott, this isn't undercover. You're just swapping down to street clothes to gather information. And those street clothes will be gym gear, so get home and get your kit or you'll have to do it in your underwear.'

Cullen winced. 'I might have to buy some workout clothes.'

Jain grinned. 'What, because you've obviously never been to a gym?'

'Aye, very good. No, my *running* gear's all sweaty. Three ten k's on the trot this week.'

'Running's a mug's game.' No two ways about it, Hunter was flexing for her benefit. 'Trouble is, Luke, I'm a member at Rock Hard.'

'Craig, that's excellent news. You'll blend right in.' Shepherd sprang away from the door and clapped his hands again. 'I don't expect a result any time soon, okay? But two people almost died. If we can get a collar, we can show those drugs pricks how to do their jobs.' He smiled at Jain. 'Present company excepted.'

'No, they are pricks, Luke.' She was smiling back. 'Total bastards.'

Cullen was going to have to be the dick here, wasn't he? 'Should we be doing that?'

'What?'

'Well, we were out picking up Rebecca thingy for—'

'Scott, she's got a name.'

'Aye, aye, but we were supposed to be tracking her down and—'

'This is top priority now. Davenport says it's the only way to clean up the streets.'

Cullen just bet Ally saw it that way and not a chance to soak up some glory for himself.

8

Hunter

The drone of the treadmills, the clanking of weights, the throb of chart dance music, the stink of sweat from the leather pads on the machines because nobody ever cleaned them after getting their sweaty backs all over them.

Aye, Hunter found it great to be back in the gym after all those days watching Cullen crunch spreadsheets and speaking to people who definitely didn't see anything, no sir.

Hunter was wearing his usual gym gear, the baggiest stuff he could find. Keep the air circulating. Long grey tracky bottoms and a blue hoodie. Like he was the dealer. Just his lime-green running shoes to indicate any money spent at all, but they looked like they'd seen better years.

Cullen, though. Christ. His trainers looked far too white. And he had one of his idiot flatmate's T-shirts, so faded that the text was illegible. Probably a stupid in-joke. Still, the shorts were a good fit, especially in the mirrors all over the place. Showed that the daft sod did actually have some muscles, even if they were all in his legs. That was running for you... And of course he made a beeline for the treadmill.

Hunter grabbed his T-shirt and tugged him back, then got in his ear. 'We're not here to run, we're here to train with the big boys.' He pointed across the massive room, past the fixed-weight machines, the kind a weed like Cullen would have to psyche himself up to even think about looking at, over to the free weights in the corner, where the muscle monsters worked out. 'See?'

A gang of big lads, all at least twice the size of even Hunter. Two stood either side as another pumped away at the bench press, the bar moving up and down with grace, even though it bowed and wobbled from how much weight was stuck on either end.

Twat.

'See those guys?' Hunter pointed at them. 'They're the idiots who are in here all day, every day.'

'Don't they have jobs?'

'If they're lucky, they'll get some modelling work.'

Cullen snarled. '*Modelling*?'

'Aye, photo shoots. Big business for lads like that. But most of the time they're in here, working out. And see the size of them? You don't get that big from protein shakes.'

'Protein what?'

'Scott, they're on steroids. And I'm guessing the Viper has either been dealing it to them or whoever has knows who the Viper is.'

Another guy stood with a similarly bulging bar bell gripped at waist height. A boxing champion's belt wrapped around him, gloves on, grunting and moaning like a Viking, then he lowered the heaving weights down to the mat, his face twisted into a grimace, then eased them back up again. Then again and again.

Romanian deadlifts. Hardcore.

He eased them down one final time and rested them on the mat, no thunk, no wobble.

A whoop of applause burst out.

'Big Rob!'

'You da *man*!'

The one who'd been bench pressing slapped the dead-lifter on the back. Nothing moved. Big Rob looked like he'd been made in a volcano. Smelted. And now he wasn't gurning from the effort, Hunter knew his face from the gym, and could now put a name to it. The few times he'd seen him, Hunter clocked him as the alpha around here, with a load of betas swarming around him. Big Rob, eh?

'Come on.' Hunter marched over and grabbed a forty-kilo kettlebell from the rack against the wall. 'What's the celebration, boys?'

'Just beat my personal best.' Big Rob wandered over and stood next to them, spraying water into his mouth from a branded bottle, one of those protein companies, but the plastic was faded off. The smell of sour sweat poured off him, drenching his cream T-shirt a muddy beige. 'Three hundred kilos, on the nose. Ten reps.'

'That include the bar?'

Rob nodded. 'Sure does, sir.'

'Impressive.' Hunter clutched his own paltry weight's handle with both hands and rested it between his legs, then thrust with his hips, driving the weight up until it swung back, then he squatted down and repeated the movement. 'I'm lucky to clear two hundred.'

'Aye?'

'Aye. But I'm talking vanilla deadlifts, not your Romanian ones.'

'Much harder starting from standing.' Another spray of water into his mouth.

Cullen picked up a kettlebell half the size of Hunter's and tried to do the same exercise. On the third swing, the kettlebell flew out of his hands.

Big Rob caught it one handed, by the handle, and swung it round. He tossed it up in the air and brought it down with a grace nothing like his size suggested. 'Steady there, my man. Can take someone's head off.' He smiled. 'Maybe not with that weight. And your stance is bollocksed.'

Cullen didn't take the bell back off him. 'Ah, you bastard.'

Hunter was at twenty reps now. He set the weight down and walked over. 'What's up?'

Cullen held up his hand and it looked like something from a crime scene, all bloody and sore. He'd torn some skin on his left hand, the palm side of the knuckles. He took the weight back from Big Rob with a nod, then rested it between his feet. Last thing he seemed to want was to start it up again. 'My fingers are *burning*.'

Big Rob was drinking water again. 'Get some gloves, man.'

'Gloves?'

'Aye.' Rob showed off his hands. Massive and stuffed into work gloves. 'Those bells are great for functional strength, but bad for manicures.'

Hunter's hands were callused from barehanded kettlebell swings.

Cullen held out his palms, soft and pale.

Big Rob grabbed them and stroked across. 'The hands of an office worker. You're new to this, aye?' He shifted his grin to smile at Hunter. 'Whereas you're not. Seen your face around.'

Hunter dropped to his hands, kicked back, did a press-up, then kicked back up again and ended with a jump. 'Aye. Been a member a couple of years.'

'Nice burpee, pal.'

'Just a warm-up.'

'Aye? You lifting weights?'

'Maybe.'

'So, you looking to get big?'

'Bigger, anyway.'

'Won't get there with pounding kettlebells and doing burpees, eh?'

Hunter repeated the burpee, then shrugged after his jump. 'I do deadlifts four times a week. Vanilla ones, unlike your Romanian ones.' He nodded behind Big Rob. 'Want to get to three hundred this year.'

'Big goal, that.'

'I've done it before.'

'Aye, but you should be doing benchpresses and bar squats, pal.' Rob walked over and lay down, then pulled the weight off the rack and started lifting, up and down, slow and steady. 'I'd ask one of you pair to spot me, but it's not like both of you together could hold even the *bar*.'

Hunter laughed it off, but he was puffing hard, now on his tenth burpee. 'So how would you get big?'

'Twenty!' Rob pushed the bar back and got up, flexing like a bugger. Under his slicked vest, he was *ripped*. Shredded. Whatever the latest term was, he was it. Not an ounce of fat. That brown leathery look you saw in muscle mags, just not oiled up. 'You're talking about for Woody Allen here, aren't you?'

Cullen arched his eyebrow. 'Charming.'

Hunter smiled at Cullen. 'Aye, he can't raise a smile, let alone a kettlebell.' Not for the first time, Cullen was the subject of a chat he was present for. The kind Hunter liked best. Hard to see him ever making the grade as a DC, but he was Hunter's way into Big Rob's head here. 'He's just starting out, but wants to get serious, really quickly.'

Big Rob slapped Cullen's arm. 'You're quite lean, Woody Allen. I'm guessing you're a fireman?'

Cullen stared hard at him, with the bright eyes of a trained liar. 'No, I work at Alba Bank.' He blew air up his face. 'And I'm just *bored*, you know? Need a hobby.' A flash of eyebrows. 'And getting ripped might help with the lassies.'

'And the laddies!' Big Rob thumped Cullen's arm, almost toppling him over like skittles. 'Maybe you need a PT.'

'A what?'

'Physical Trainer.' Rob was flexing again. 'I mean, I

used to be a streak of piss like you, but you need a lot of whey protein to be anything other than a fat slob.'

'So you're offering to train me?'

'Sure am.' Rob walked over to them, grabbing them both in his massive arms. He took a drink from a second bottle, something green that smelled like it had come out of someone. 'Know the best way to get big?' He was whispering. 'Supplements. And pills.'

'What kind of pills? Steroids?'

'Not steroids, mate.'

'But you do get steroids, aye?'

'Mate, steroids are yesterday's business. SARMs are where it's at.'

'SARMs?'

'No idea what it stands for. Could be changing my gender, who knows, but this stuff I get is off the charts.'

'And it's legal?'

'Ish.'

'You got any?'

'How much do you want?'

Bingo.

9

Bain

I switch off the engine and let out the mother of all yawns. One of those ones that feels like it could go on until next Tuesday. At least. Been a hell of a long day already and it's only quarter past eleven. Christ on a bike, eh? And my guts are churning something rotten. Two haggis and tattie scone bagels is maybe a bit too aggressive with my constitution, but it's tough to turn them down when they're just sitting there.

I pop open my door and let the freezing air in. 'This city.' I shake my head. 'Swear it's about five degrees colder than Glasgow.'

'You haven't got used to it after all this time, eh?' Sharon McNeill's in the passenger seat, face as sour as if she'd drunk a pint of curdled milk. Big lassie, not that there's anything wrong with that, but she can handle herself. And the look she's giving me right now, Christ. Hardest part of this gig is I didn't get to choose my detective sergeants. 'Five years now, isn't it?'

'Just over, aye.' I step out into the pissing rain and I swear it's like the water's making a beeline for my moustache. Should really shave the thing off, but I've taken so much stick for it over the years, don't want the pricks to think they've won. It's like a badge of honour, isn't it? I trudge through the rain and this coat isn't exactly putting up much of a fight against the elements.

Rock Hard Gym, all lit up in glowing lights, way brighter than it should be. I mean, it's like in that *Blade Runner* film, where everything's all dark but the signs are super-bright. Got the Definitive Cut or Final Cut or whatever to watch on Blu-Ray, one among very many sitting in a pile by the fancy new telly that's still in its box.

Anyway, the place is deserted, stuck on a back street at the arse end of the Cowgate. No matter how much of a rip-off Edinburgh is for business, there's always wee places like this burrowed away in the ground.

Normally, I'd let the lady go first but bugger that, it's freezing and I'm dripping wet, so I charge into the place before McNeill.

Fuck me with a lightning rod, it's even colder inside,

like the air conditioning's turned up to eleven. Or down to eleven. Can never remember which.

Place has all that stripped-back shite you get nowadays. Rather than plastering the walls, it's just bare stone. Edinburgh stone, so damp and reeking. Not much in the way of partitions, either, so I can see a lassie hammering the treadmill, her ponytail swinging behind her.

Place absolutely mings of caramel-y sweat and I can feel the bass thrumming in the soles of my feet. Christ.

Some clanking of weights come from the back. Meaning there's a bunch of muscle boys working out in here. Hence the pong of BO. Dirty bastards never clean after themselves.

The door rattles behind us and McNeill slides in, shaking off her brolly and catching us in the face with her spray. Doesn't even apologise. Didn't even offer me a place under it. She grins at us. 'You look like you're going to work out in here.'

'More your scene, eh?'

'Just because I've got a Personal Trainer, doesn't—'

'Too much testosterone for you?'

She sighs at us, then switches it to a smile, like that'll deter us. 'Something like that.'

Not enough, more like. I stroll on up to the counter and lean against the desk. Fancy green thing made of glass, right up at standing height. No sign of a bell or anything. 'Shop!'

A machine stops whirring and someone thumps down to the floor. The lassie on the running machine walks over to us, sweat absolutely pishing off her. Hair looks dry as my arse after I've wiped, mind. 'Can I help you, sir?'

'Only if you work here.'

'I do.'

'Well, then.' I take out my warrant card and hold it out. 'DI Brian Bain. This is DS Sharon McNeill.' I wait to let the lassie nod at her, not that she's giving me anything. 'Know where I can find an Alexander Drake?'

'He a member here?'

'No, we gather he works here.'

She doesn't look like she gives a shite about being caught out in a lie. 'Right, so you mean Sandy?'

'Aye.' Who knows? Who cares? 'Been to his flat, but no sign of the lad.'

'This in connection to that court case?'

I just raise my eyebrows.

She sits on a stool behind the desk and grabs a towel off the floor. Dirty cow. It's smeared with fluff and lint. 'Told me about it. Some lassie was lying about him raping her.'

Not my case, darling, but I let it slide. She's obviously tight with the raping wee bastard, so better play along. 'Something like that.'

She runs her towel through her long hair and bunches it up over her skinny shoulder. 'Sandy's been to hell and back over that, you know?'

'Can well imagine. So, is he here?'

'Nope. He's in court. Like you just said.'

'Well, see, that's the thing. He got let go for the rest of the day. Then my boss told me to find out if he had anything to do with the witness against him not showing. Like I said, we've just been to his flat. And he wasn't there. He ever talk about any friends that he'd visit in a time of need?'

Shakes her head at us. Christ, she's not giving me anything to work with here. 'Could ask around for you?'

'That'd be smashing.' I drum my fingers on the desk, like I'm thinking everything through. 'You got any staff records here?'

'Why would that help?'

I look around the gym. 'Place like this, I imagine you lot are PTs as well as working the desk, right?'

'Right?'

'Well, if he's been a PT to someone whose name I or DS McNeill recognise, then that'd be a red flag. Especially if it's recently. Capiche?'

She scowls at us, then drops the towel back on the floor. 'I understand, but why should I help?'

'Because he wasn't exactly straight with you. Mr Drake did rape that woman. Becky Crawford. There's DNA evidence.'

Her shoulders collapsed. 'Shite.'

'So, anyone he might've been associated with, we'd like to speak to them.'

She's nodding now, but looks a wee bit shocked. 'It's all on the computer through the back.'

'Mind showing me?'

'Got a warrant?'

'No.'

'But you're not leaving unless I check, are you?'

'Right. Wouldn't want to let your muscles cool down too much from your run, eh?'

'I get it. Come on.' She stands up and she's actually a wee bit taller than yours truly. Still not as big as McNeill, mind, who is chatting some shite to her as we walk through the place.

Now, there's a lassie who needs a nickname. Sharon McNeill. Everybody in my team's got a really solid nickname, but she's managed to escape it so far.

Well, I don't have one. Unless Bri counts. And those sneaky wee shites might have one for us that I don't know. But you can't control what people say behind your back, can you?

Given it's still early, this place is pretty busy. Daft laddies by the bench press grunting and grinding away.

Something clatters and someone shouts something. Might be a nickname. Aye, it must be.

See? They're everywhere. Terms of affection, endearment, you choose what word you use, but it's how you build a team that wins, that achieves great things. Camaraderie.

The reception lassie stops by a door and opens a cupboard, barely a metre deep. A computer sits on a desk that you have to stand up to type on. What's the point in that? Waste of energy. She types away at the machine. Still don't have her name, which is something I need to rectify. Christ. She's taking her time, likes.

'Reading *War and Peace* there or something?'

She looks around at us. 'The owner likes to keep meticulous records. Finding stuff is more an art than a science.'

'That right, aye?' Doesn't look like she's wiping anything, but I've no idea what wiping anything would look like, eh? That computer must be older than me.

And my guts are burning… 'Here, anywhere I could go for a jobbie?'

The lassie looks around at us like I'm five. 'Changing rooms.' She points over to the side.

'Excellent. Thanks.' I charge off quick smart as this one isn't going to wait. The door swings open and I take a quick look. Three numpties sitting by the lockers, and a row of stalls on the right. Bingo. I tear into the first one and drop my drawers, then my arse onto the cold seat, then drop my guts into the pan.

Bloody hell.

That's the bambers, I tell you. The surge of relief. Must be like bungie jumping or diving out of a plane with a parachute, whatever that's called.

And it's all over, bar the screaming. I bunch off some bog paper from the wee box machine and wipe away, though it's dry as hell down there.

Makes us think about that bog roll the old boy swears about, the medicated stuff that doesn't so much wipe as smear it all about. Izal or something.

'So, you take these, you'll get a lot bigger.'

Woah, hang on a wee minute here.

'I mean, you have to train your nuts off every day, but these things will help you push past your upper limit and will let you train for hours. And you'll get massive with the right programme.'

A pause.

'You boys smell that?' The first voice.

'Aye, like a dog's been in here.' Another pause. 'So, how much?'

'Ten quid for a sample box.'

'And after that?'

'We'll come to an arrangement. But you'll get solid results just from that little lot.'

Another pause. 'What do you think, Craig?'

'I'd do it, aye.'

Drug deal. Just stumbled onto it. In the name of the wee man.

I drop the last of the bog paper into the pan and stand up. Better not flush in case they hear me.

'Right, well, here's a tenner.'

Got my cameraphone out now, primed for a photo. I point it over at the lockers and ease the door open. Snap, snap, snap. Money one way, gear the other. And I. Catch. It. All.

Daft bastards.

'Police!' I hold out my warrant card. 'You three are under arrest.'

They all swing around to look at us.

One's a scrawny wee boy-band prick, but the other two are muscle monsters. Shite. Haven't quite thought this through.

Bugger it. When in the lion's den, act like the lion. Or something.

'Now, I hope you boys don't think about running away from me.'

The absolutely massive one does, aye. He darts right towards me and spears me against the door. It flies open and I fly free, stumbling back into the bog I've just left, cracking my spine against the wall.

Left foot down in the pan, right on top of the jobbie I've just dropped.

'Christ's sake!'

The big bastard is standing in the doorway, arms raised in a boxer's stance.

I whip out my baton and lash out at the prick, catching him in the throat.

He chokes like he's swallowed a monkey nut whole, shell and all, and goes down.

Give his vest a good rub with my foot, clearing most of my dung off the smooth soles. Prick's not going anywhere.

But his mates have.

Ah, shite.

I shoot back out into the gym and, in the name of the wee man, the little boy-band prick is running around the gym, followed by McNeill.

Doesn't notice his shoe laces are untied, mind. He stumbles and she kicks his feet out from underneath him, then McNeill goes to town on him, pushing him face first into the floor.

The receptionist is standing next to us, mouth hanging wide open. 'Christ, what's that smell?'

My shoe is what! Christ!

But enough of this nonsense. 'Sunshine, you're under arrest. You and your big mate in the cludgie through there. Dealing and buying controlled substances. Tut tut.'

But the wee boy-band wanker looks up at us and

whispers, 'I'm a cop. Acting DC Scott Cullen.'

10

Cullen

Arrested.

Christ's sake.

Cullen stood by a purple Mondeo and looked around the car park. No sign of Hunter. Typical — he'd always bugger off at the first sign of trouble.

The female officer who'd taken Cullen down was ducking Big Rob's head, forcing him into the back seat of an orange Fiat Punto. The man mountain looked broken and bruised.

Cullen looked at the older cop, with his headmaster moustache and Hitler haircut, a greasy side parting. The one who'd done that to Big Rob. And the one who absolutely reeked, like he'd shat himself. 'I told you, I'm a cop.'

'You're lying, son.'

'No. We're working and we don't want to blow our operation.'

'Christ's sake. Get in.' He grabbed Cullen's shoulder and pushed him in the back of the Mondeo.

Cullen let him do it and sat on the seat. The car was filled with crushed cans of syrupy energy drink. The door slammed, a bit too loud.

Moustache got behind the wheel and swivelled around, lashing bitter coffee breath over Cullen's face, a pleasant break from the smell of shit. 'Son, you need to think this through.' He widened his eyes. 'If I'm being generous, and I believe you, and you were trying to arrest that big lump, then that's fine. *If* that's the case, then you need to play along to maintain whatever cover you're trying to keep here with your tight shorts.'

'Of course it's the truth.'

'*But*, if you're lying, then I'll add this to your charge list.'

'I work for DS Luke—'

'Lie.'

'My badge number is—'

'Show us your card, dickhead.'

'My warrant card's in my locker.'

'Then we'll find it. But I don't think it exists.'

Cullen needed to play along with his game. He focused on him and it was like staring at an oncoming train. 'Okay, I'll play along, but you owe me your name.'

'DI Brian Bain.'

'CID? Drugs? What?'

'The former. Based down in Leith Walk.'

'Who's your DCI?'

'You cheeky wee bastard.' Bain shook his head. 'Jim Turnbull.'

'Right.' Cullen had no idea who he was, but then he didn't know many cops above DS level.

'You sitting there acting like you know him. Cheeky sod. You could pretend he took a training course you were on once.'

'Right. He did.'

'Very pleased for you, sunshine.'

'Look, I'm based in St Leonards. Get my warrant card and—'

'Never heard of warrant cards being faked, eh?'

'Then I suggest you call DI Ally Davenport to verify my identity.'

'Never heard of him.'

'What about DS Shepherd?'

He frowned. 'Big Luke?'

'You know him?'

Bain was beaming wide. 'Why didn't you say?' He got out and hollered over. 'Sharon, can you call DS

Shepherd? Think we've got two of his suspects.' The door clicked shut.

Cullen sat back in and folded his arms, waiting.

'You get him?'

Cullen jumped and hit his head off the roof.

Hunter was sitting in the passenger seat, craning his neck around. 'Well, did you get Big Rob?'

'Jesus, Craig, how did you—'

'Tell me you got him.'

'Aye, he did.'

'Good.'

The driver door opened and Bain got in, but left the door open. 'Son, you've got ten seconds to get out of my car before I arrest you.'

Cullen leaned forward. 'He's my DC.'

Bain switched his gaze between them, before settling on Cullen. 'Thought you said *you* were a DC?'

'Training. Acting. Whatever you want to call it.'

Bain huffed out a sigh. 'So Big Luke's got you two fannies working a gym? Sounds like bollocks to me. Suspect Big Luke arrested you two a while ago and he's the name you know.' He jabbed a finger into Hunter's bulging arm. 'What's your story, then?'

'It's a long one. Short version is we've got a lead on a dealer here. We were trying to get some steroids, see if we can find him. Found someone willing to sell us some stuff without much asking. Stands to reason it's either him, or he knows who's dealing heroin in there.'

'So you're spending a ton of time trying to snare some daft sod over *steroids*?'

'No, it's heroin. The bodybuilding gear might be connected.'

'Heroin?' Bain winced. 'You two drugs squad?'

Hunter shook his head. 'CID.'

'So why are you investigating drugs?'

'It's in conjunction with DI Wilkinson's team. He's on secondment over there. Him and DC Jain. You know Paul?'

'That big wanker. Right.'

'You believe us, or what?'

'Let's just say you seem seasoned enough to be partnered up with an ADC to train and be a good laddie. And being a bit more savvy on the street than this Cullen chump here, you slipped out when that big bastard slammed us into a stall?' He thumbed behind him again. 'Whereas your pal here got caught.'

'Pretty much.' Hunter's nostrils twitched. 'What's that smell?'

'Never you mind. What's your name?'

'Craig Hunter. And the big bastard who slammed you in the toilets is—'

'That sounds like a gay thing.'

'Your words.' Hunter was smirking. 'Your guy's name is Big Rob. Robert Woodhead, I think.'

'You think?'

'Could be Woodford or something similar.' Hunter held his gaze. 'Mind telling us who you are?'

'I'm the lead DI at Leith Walk. Jim Turnbull's had a favour called in and been asked to find the defendant. Hence us being here.'

'The *defendant*?'

'You are aware of the legal system, aye? They teach you it at Tulliallan on your first bloody day.'

'No need to be a smart arse.'

'I've every need. Was it your boss who let a chief witness not show up at court?'

Hunter frowned. 'DI Davenport, aye. Why?'

'So, when the witness didn't show, court was adjourned until they found her. Right? Trouble is, he was remanded in custody because you don't give bail to scum like him. But when they adjourned the trial, his bloody lawyer argued for bail. Stringent conditions, mind, but Campbell McLintock knows his onions. And he'd surrendered his passport, but nothing actually stopped him from reporting said passport lost and getting a new one. Only for him to bugger off.'

'So you've been asked to find him?'

'Something like that. Alexander Drake. Know him?'

Cullen looked at Hunter, frowning. 'Drake could be the Viper?'

Hunter shrugged. 'Maybe.'

'What you two on about?'

'Almost lost two homeless women to super-strong heroin this morning. Tracked it to a smack dealer who we think works out of here.'

'Christ's sake. Got three deaths related to that.'

'Sorry to hear it. But that's all on the word of—'

Bain's door opened wide and DS McNeill poked her head into the car. 'Spoke to Luke. It all checks out.'

Bain smoothed down his moustache, examining Hunter and Cullen for a few seconds each. 'Well, the pair of you can bugger off.'

Cullen frowned at him. 'That's it?'

'Aye.'

'Cheers.' Cullen smiled at McNeill. 'Commiserations on having to work for him, by the way.'

Bain laughed. 'She's learning from the best cop in Lothian and Borders, sunshine.'

Hunter smirked. 'That'll be Jim Turnbull, aye?'

'*Me*, you fanny.' Bain reached over and grabbed hold of Hunter. 'But your collar's in her car, so we'll have to take you back to ours so we don't blow your cover with that big lump over there. Don't want Luke losing his drugs prosecution on account of your incompetence.'

Cullen looked around at Hunter, then back to Bain. 'Or you could let us go now.'

'I can't let you go, you stupid bastard. You were buying drugs off him!'

'So, pretend it's a mistake. A misunderstanding. Let us go. All of us.'

'He smashed me in the bogs!'

McNeill was frowning. 'He what?'

'Not you as well.'

Hunter raised his palms, callused over like tree bark. 'We both need intel off Big Rob. He might know where this Alex Drake's gone. I'm betting he knows who the Viper is and if it's Drake. Either way, we need to find the Viper before anyone else buys his heroin.'

Bain drummed at the steering wheel a few times, then looked around at McNeill. 'What do you think?'

She shrugged. 'Does it matter what I think?'

'Suppose not.' Bain snorted. 'Right, you can go. Take that big fanny too. And I suppose I'll see you at this Christmas party tonight.'

Hunter opened his door. 'You might want to change your shoes first.'

11

Hunter

Big Rob was fuming. Slamming his gym shoes into his locker, the din rattling around the changing room. He was stripped to the waist. Not even a roll of flab, though he moved like a sloth. All that muscle weighed. He bent down to hoik his shorts off and stood up, his ding-dong right in Hunter's face.

Hunter had to look away. 'Christ, man. I don't want to talk into the mic.'

Rob looked down at his cock and laughed. 'Sorry. Just...' He sat down with a sigh. Everything hung loose, except for his muscles. 'That was a close shave, man.'

Just like his pubes. And his body. Not even a strip of hair on his belly, no circles around his nipples.

Hunter looked up at the ceiling. 'Aye, very close.' Just like Rob was right then. 'What did she ask you?'

'She just sweated me. Asked where I got the 'roids from.'

'You tell them anything?'

'I'm a very careful man. I've only got enough for me here. Nothing like the quantity a dealer would need. Always knew at some point they'd take me to their cop shop, make me sweat. So not giving them an inch.'

'Aye, that's what I was fearing, hence me pissing off.'

Rob narrowed his eyes, and Hunter looked up at the ceiling again. 'Why did you run?'

'Because. I slipped out when you attacked that cop.'

'I know. Just asking why?'

'Well, got a few arrest warrants out.' Hunter held out a hand. 'Nothing dodgy. Just went AWOL from the army.'

Rob laughed. 'You too?'

'Wanker of a Staff Sergeant had it in for me.'

'Tell me about it.' Rob sighed, deep and desperate. 'They do you too?'

'No. And I know bugger all. Except for your roids. And you seem like a good guy.'

'Rob.' He took his hand away from cupping his balls and thrust it out to Hunter. 'Rob Woodhead.'

'Craig Hunter. I'll not shake that after where it's been.'

'Aye. Good point.'

'So, you work out here a lot?'

'Every day, except a Saturday. That's when I flob out on the sofa, watch some shite on the telly, eat junk food. Two pizzas, a Nando's chicken, bag of tortillas, twelve cans of beer. Feed my body, then burn it away the rest of the week.'

'That work for you?'

'Aye, man.' Big Rob pulled out a pair of trousers and stepped into them, commando-style. 'And I do OMAD the rest of the time.'

'OMAD?'

'One Meal A Day. All my calories in one go. Keeps me lean.' He slapped his belly. 'You serious about bulking up?'

'Thinking about getting into flexing, aye.'

'Tough gig. Used to be popular, but it's tough to make ends meet now, like. Have to have a big job to get in there.'

'A big job? I thought you'd have to train full-time?'

'No way, man. The gear you need? Costs a *bomb* now. Need to earn a lot or have sponsorship to pay for it. Like your pal.'

'My pal?'

'The banker. Woody Allen.'

'Right. Aye, like him. Too much money, eh?'

'Aye. Seems like a runner. Where'd he go, by the way?'

'Cops took him.'

'Shit. Why?'

'Cheeky bastard. Said something he shouldn't have.'

'You guys close?'

'Not really. His sister's shagging my brother.'

'Got you.'

'You're lucky you didn't get taken in for your impression of The Rock on the arsehole with the moustache.'

Rob rubbed his forehead. 'Well, he clattered me with a truncheon so it's all fair in love and war, eh?'

'Guess so.' Hunter pulled his gym top up over his head and tossed it into his bag.

Rob was checking him out. 'You've got a good frame, have to say. But you've got a lot of work to do.'

'So, those SARMs would help?'

'Like nobody's business.' Big Rob tapped his nose. 'Thing is, what I was selling you wasn't them. Reason the cops let us go.'

'So what was it?'

'Mexican diet pills. Clean you out like nobody's business. All those calories I have every Saturday, well, let's just say they're not in my system very long.'

'Got you.'

'Boosts my metabolism too. Helps my body process protein.' Rob flexed, cupping his palms together. 'See?'

'Aye, aye.'

'And I'm not a dealer.'

'So why sell us those pills?'

'Thought you were asking me so you could grass on me. Get me in the shit.'

'No, man.' Hunter felt like this was getting away from him. Cullen was outside, ready to come in and give them another angle, but he really should be able to get something from this chump. Something now. 'Just want to get big. And quickly. That's it.'

'Right, right.' Rob tugged on a rugby shirt that was two sizes too small. Looked like he was going to tear it in half. His nipples were like bullets. 'Okay, so I know how to get a bit of everything. Test, deca, winny, dbol, oxys, sus. You name it.'

'And if I wanted to get a bit of something?'

'Then I'd introduce you to this guy.'

'Got a name?'

'The Viper. Big guy, from Penicuik I think. Works out as much as me.' Rob frowned. 'Anyway, he's into all the science. The latest steroids, Mexican drug pills, hydration strategies. Those SARMs. You name it.'

'He trains here?'

'Aye. Think he might be a member of staff here, but it's hard to figure out who is and who isn't, you know. Called Sandy.'

And Sandy might be Alex Drake, the guy Bain and McNeill were looking for.

Hunter sat back and folded his arms. 'He the one who's been dealing heroin?'

'Heroin?'

'Before I came back, I heard the cops asking my pal about it. Woody Allen. Said two women are at the ERI from dodgy smack they got from someone called The Viper. Other people are dead too.'

'Shite.' Big Rob collapsed back against the locker. And he wasn't speaking.

Hunter had two options here. Get Cullen to come in, try to play the "pigs were all over me" card. Or... 'I'm a cop.'

Rob jerked upright, looking ready to fight. 'What?'

'DC Craig Hunter.' Hunter raised his hands, trying to placate him. He'd seen Big Rob in action and it wasn't pretty.

A meaty finger jabbed towards Hunter. 'You lying arsehole!'

'I'm sorry. But, for what it's worth, you got that copper good and proper. Nice work.'

'Why did you lie to me?' Rob looked like he was going to punch Hunter. 'Trying to snare me?'

'What makes you think that?'

'Well, you could be working with those two.'

'Mate, I got them to agree to drop your assault on DI Bain. I know DS McNeill. She's a ball buster, but she's someone I can deal with.' Hunter sat back against the locker. 'I've told you the truth about a lot of things, okay? That guy we're after, The Viper? We have it from a reliable source,' he felt himself cough, 'that he's been selling a batch of super-strong heroin that's killing people. Bain and McNeill are looking for someone called Alexander Drake who works here. He's a defendant in a rape case.'

Rob looked over, eyes narrowing. 'Rape?'

Hunter nodded. 'Seems to have put the frighteners on the victim. Now he's run off and the case is falling apart.'

Big Rob flared his nostrils. 'Christ.'

'My assumption is he's been dealing steroids or SARMs or whatever to you and the other bodybuilders here. But I also think he's been dealing heroin. And he's a rapist. So. If you know anything about him, now's the time.'

'And you want me to spill in return for helping me?'

'Look, I told McNeill that they can trust you, but I don't know... maybe *I* can't. I mean, I don't really know you, do I? I've just seen you in the gym. Worked out a bit together. That time you spotted my benching. I could say to them that you're—'

'It's not the Viper who's the big man here.' Rob folded his arms. 'He just gets stuff from him.'

'Wouldn't mind speaking to The Viper or to the big man. Either works.'

Rob lifted his shoulder. 'Aye, good luck with Sandy. Got a text from him, said he's on his way to Chile.'

Hunter felt a ton of bricks land on his shoulder. '*Chile*?'

'Aye.'

'He's fleeing the country?'

'Well, Chile's the other side of the world, so aye.'

'Did he say when?'

'Took off an hour ago.' Rob checked his watch. 'Flight from Newcastle to Buenos Aires.'

'That's in Argentina.'

Rob shrugged. 'Same difference.'

Hunter collapsed against the locker. They'd lost. Let a rapist escape. And Chile or Argentina, whichever it was. Even if we could find him, nobody is going to authorise the expense to return him from there. Cross any borders you like over there. Hunter knew a few ex-army guys who worked in Brazil and Argentina. Despite the cities being modern, it was still the Wild West out in the countryside. And there was a lot of it. Lot of cattle work, the kind of anonymous cash-in-hand work where questions weren't even thought of, let alone asked.

Hunter locked eyes with Big Rob. 'I need to know who this big man is. Who Drake buys his drugs from.'

'Okay. There's a guy here. Don't know his name, but he's a runner type. Pounds the treadmill for a couple of hours. And he's been dealing from his locker.'

Hunter looked around the room, three sides stacked high with lockers. 'You know which one?'

12

Bain

Trick with big bastards like this one is to take the lead, to own the situation, so I grab him in a big hug, even though he's almost twice my size. 'Luke, my man.' Head over his shoulder, looking around the car park, but there's no sign of the other big bugger. Just a few motors and a shitload of wind. Bit of grit catches us in the mouth. And these new shoes are already scraping at my heels. Christ on a bike. 'Been way too long.'

'Nowhere near long enough.' Shepherd shoves my arms out of the way and steps out of my big manly hug. Getting them on the back foot is all part of it, though. He's massive, in a different way to that big bastard who speared me. Big like he loves his pies. 'So, this is on the level?'

'So I gather.' And I nod over at where Hunter should be, but isn't. 'Your lad got the lead, Luke.'

'Hmm.'

'Boys.' Hunter jogs towards us, out of nowhere. He's in his civvies, not that baggy gym gear he had on before. 'Thanks for getting here so quickly.'

Shepherd thumbs behind him, past his clapped-out Vauxhall. 'Craig, the station's just five minutes that way. Even I could walk that distance in no time.'

'Aye, aye, just wondering if you got the warrant?'

Shepherd reaches into his jacket pocket with a sly grin. 'Ally says your arse is on the line here, Craig.'

'Always is.'

Christ, I'm losing control of this.

I'm supposed to be the bloody DI here, not Shepherd.

So I clap Hunter on the arm. 'Good work, Craig. Flirting with the muscle boy in the changing rooms clearly paid off.'

He looks at me like he wants to batter the living shite out of me in a phone box. 'Wasn't flirting.'

'Aye you were, you big bugger. And I took the measure of the boy in the cludgie, too.' I give him the grin of the Banter Lord and a nod too, for good measure. 'Anyway. Where's your wee pal?'

Shepherd narrows his eyes at us. 'Sent him on an errand. Some call him the donkey as he's good at running around.'

'Could do with something to eat. Too late?' I hold out my brand spanking new Sony Ericsson phone. Smashing thing it is. Shiny. Can even get my email on it. 'Shall I call him?'

'Not that kind of errand.'

'Right.' Feel a bit of a wally with this prop in my hands, but hey ho. 'DS McNeill called us on my way over. She's got in touch with the airline. One David John Smith flew from Newcastle to Amsterdam on the one o'clock flight, heading to Buenos Aires, apparently. Thing is, if you look at the boy's passport scan, it's the face of Alexander Nicholas Drake.'

Shepherd doesn't seem too impressed with my bling phone, and less so with the news. 'So he left the court and went straight to the airport then flew under an assumed identity?'

'About the size of it.'

Shepherd nods at the gym. 'Meanwhile you just happened to be here, seeing if he'd gone to work?'

'No, Luke. We'd been to his flat first.'

'Didn't you have his passport in custody?'

'We had *a* passport, aye. Trouble is, guys like that have many, many passports. Must've had one on him at court, then when *your* lassie didn't show up, he could bugger off down to Newcastle. Someone probably drove him, so we could—'

'Okay, so what about—'

'Got a European Arrest Warrant pending, Luke. You know as well as I do that those things are a nightmare at the best of times. Time isn't on our side here. He'll probably sleep in the terminal in the 'Dam tonight, then get the plane first thing tomorrow. Face it, mate, we've lost him.'

Shepherd grimaces. Maybe he knows this is his bollocks up. 'Another rapist walks away scot free, Brian. This isn't good.'

'No, but thanks to Craig and his pal, we can maybe do some good here.' I barge between the big lumps and head inside the gym.

Place is much busier than earlier. Dance music blasts out, just at that point where you'd be unable to drown it out over your headphones, no matter how loud you have the volume "The Best of Hall and Oates" playing.

Cracking work-out music, I tell you. Gets you pumping.

I mosey on up to the desk and rest the search warrant on the desk. 'Police, need to access a locker here.'

The same lassie as earlier looks up at us, but doesn't recognise us. 'A warrant?'

I run my finger over the page, signed by some chump called Davenport in time-honoured tradition. No blame attaching to me here. 'Number forty-six in the gents. As soon as you can.'

'You know the lockers aren't allocated to members, right?'

'Right. Gather this one is permanently occupied.'

'Okay. And obviously I can't go in there with you.'

'But you've got the key, aye?'

'I do.'

'And is there a male member of staff on?'

'The cleaner.'

'Well, how about you send him in with the key.' I take the warrant back and pocket it. 'I'll see him in there.' And I charge off through the gym, past a bunch of laddies standing by the water cooler. They part like the Red Sea and shut up. Maybe talking about drugs, or just each other's techniques. Who cares? I slide into the changing rooms and it reeks in there like nobody's flushed since my earlier escapade.

Just my luck that forty-six is right in the bloody corner. Top row of the three. Hard to get to and I have to stand up on the bench. At least these spare shoes have been worn in enough to not hurt like buggery.

The bastard thing is shut, which is good. Preserves the evidence.

Hunter and Shepherd join us in there. Swear, the

two of them are keeping their distance. Almost like they want this to reflect on me. And badly. Not like they're the types to defer to a DI.

The cleaner lumbers in. Boy has as much flab as muscle, I tell you. Not much taller than yours truly, and he's growling and grunting at everyone in the room.

I hop down off the bench and let him in to the corner. 'You got the key?'

'I got the secret, aye.' He grins at Shepherd. 'But you know these—'

'—aren't allocated to members, aye.' I try to make eye contact, but he's not looking at us. 'Seems like someone's not got their twenty pee coin back and have it on a permanent rental. So just let us in, son.'

'*Son*.' He shakes his head, grinning. 'I'm as old as you, pal.' He pulls out a massive keyring, like he's working at Bar-L. 'Forty-six, aye?'

'Aye. Had to be the one up there, eh?'

'Tell us about it.' But he's not shifting much, just rattling through his keys.

'You have any idea who's pinched that one?'

'None at all. Just clean it, mate. Why are you interested?'

'Long story. You going to open it or what?'

'Aye, fine.' He launches himself up onto the bench with the grace of a gymnast, just without any of that flouncing shite, then slots the key in the lock and twists.

I gesture at Hunter and Shepherd to join me and actually witness the evidence being found. Christ. Pair of useless fannies.

At least Shepherd has a camera on him, taking photos of it.

'Cheers, pal.' I nudge the cleaner out of the way and get in there myself, snapping on my blue gloves.

Bingo.

Bags of pills. Everywhere. All shapes and colours. I grab the camera off Shepherd and snap a couple of shots inside the thing. 'Looks like a bag of E. Some speed. Possibly coke. And Christ knows what else.'

'Steroids and the rest.' Hunter's on the bench, between me and the big cleaner lad. Christ, the load that wood is taking right now. 'And that's heroin.' He grabs a block and passes it over. 'Could be the smack we're looking for.

Wait a second.

Three Ziploc bags sitting at the front. First one is filled with cash wrapped around the maroon of a passport.

I take it out and ease the connector open, then flip through the pages until I get a face of a wee toerag with spiked hair, name of Kenny Falconer.

13

Cullen

Cullen took the next right and hit the same bloody door. Storage.

Christ's sake!

Of all the things he'd done that day, like getting chased around a gym by a DS, managing to get lost in the Mortuary had to be right up there. Or right down there. How could he expect his tenure to be made permanent if he couldn't find the Mortuary in Leith Walk station's basement? Still, three building's width and no windows, so no landmarks to follow like the Elm Bar over the road.

Wait. A voice, rattling down the corridor.

'I mean, you could say that, Ally. Aye.'

Cullen didn't recognise it, but the name... Hopefully it was Ally Davenport, so he followed it to the conclusion.

A mortuary, for sure, and not a storage cupboard.

Ally Davenport faced away from the door, head bowed, checking his phone and shaking it like doing so would fix whatever was wrong with it.

Another man stood opposite him, wearing a gown and a cheeky grin. Silver-threaded hair and shaggy with it, like it hadn't all agreed which way it was being parted. Presumably the pathologist.

A body on the slab in the middle. Female. Young. Pale. Dead. Shite.

It was one of Happy Jack's wives.

Cullen groaned.

The probable pathologist looked over at Cullen, did the up and down, then his face settled into a grin. 'Can I help you, Young Skywalker?'

'Got a message for DI Davenport.'

Davenport shot around and focused on Cullen. 'Ah, Scott. You okay?'

'Not really.' Cullen stayed as far away from the body as he could. 'I hadn't heard.'

'About what?'

'That one of Happy Jack's wives died.'

'His *wives*?' Davenport was frowning. 'Ah, right. Aye, Luke told me. No, she didn't pull through. Dr Yule and team tried their best, but… Sometimes we just can't save them.'

'Right.' All that hassle to get her there, just for her to end up here. Cullen had felt like a hero, but really, he'd let her down. Maybe not as badly as her parents, siblings, family members, teachers. But still. 'It's sad.'

'Isn't it just?' The pathologist held out a gloved hand, about five metres too far away to shake. 'Professor James Deeley, at your service, Young Skywalker.' He went back to his dissection with a deep frown. 'Bit of a shame I'm only thinking of that one now. Could've used it on Big Luke, but no. I feel like I jumped the gun in calling him the Lord, as he is my Shepherd.'

Davenport snorted, but it seemed to be more in derision than humour. He turned away from Deeley and folded his arms. 'How did the obbo at the gym go?'

'Luke's been trying to call you, sir. Needs you to sign a warrant.'

Davenport rolled his eyes. 'When's the raid?'

'About half an hour ago.'

'One of them, eh?' Davenport smirked. 'Right, aye. This new phone's been going tonto. No reception down here and when I get some, it's just a load of nonsense from Bain.'

Deeley laughed. 'That absolute wanker.'

'Right.' Cullen handed him the sheet of paper and a pen. 'Luke's upstairs, strategising.'

'Is he now?' Davenport pressed a button and put his phone to his ear. 'Buggering buggering hell.' He sighed. 'Scott, can you get up there and tell him the blood toxicology on her,' he gestured at the body, 'has confirmed this is definitely the same smack as Bain's cases.'

14

Bain

Shepherd's powering along the corridor in St Leonard's like he owns this place. Hands in pockets, stomping his feet hard. 'Hate this station.'

'We can swap, if you like.' I stop but don't open the door just yet. 'Hear Leith Walk's a bit of a mess, though.'

'Right. Takes us months to find our way around the Mortuary. Like a maze down there.'

'You don't miss the Cowgate?'

'Like a limb, Brian. Used to love going there, great excuse to bugger off from the Incident Room and clear my head. Now anyone can find me downstairs. And Deeley... He just gets worse.'

'Doesn't he just.' Deeley, what a fanny. I open the Incident Room door and the noise hits us. Like being back home. Sod Leith Walk, this is where it's at.

'Good morning, Lothian and Borders. How can I help?'

Ah, old Mags. Still got the patter, hasn't she?

I set off across the room like *I* own the place. When I'm done, I will. 'You know who this Kenny Falconer guy is?'

Shepherd shakes his head. 'I'm as in the dark as you, Brian.'

'Great.' I open the office door marked Davenport and hold it for Shepherd, then follow him in. Christ, he's *massive*.

Wee Chantal is sitting there. Not seen her for a year or two. 'Hey, Luke.'

I sit next to her. 'Don't I get a welcome?'

'Nope.' Charming. She sits there, an ice queen. 'Thought it was the Viper you were after?'

'Was.' Big metal lump in the chair's digging into my right buttock. 'Alexander Drake. But he's buggered off to Argie Bargie.'

'Disappointing.'

'Isn't it? Seems like he was working for this Kenny Falconer lad, who was dealing everything out of his locker. Should see the things he's got in there.' I shift, but that lump seems to follow me. 'Found a few knives.'

She raises her eyebrows. 'Well, you'll be glad to know that I've been doing your work for you. Turns out Kenny Falconer is on our radar.'

I try to look at her laptop, but she's blocking the view and the lump is itching my jacksy something rotten, so I get to my feet and offer the chair to Luke.

'Trouble is, we had Falconer pegged as a junior. Have him prime suspect for a few knife murders, but nothing the PF will touch with a bargepole.'

Christ, feels like it's broken the skin. 'So he's some kind of hitman?'

'Aye. Seems like he's stepping up, though. Taking on a bigger role in the organisation.' Jain's back at her laptop. 'Okay, so from what we know, Falconer runs a bookshop in Gorgie.'

Shepherd scowls at her, then at me. 'A bookshop? Like, selling novels?'

'More like a few tatty paperbacks and a *lot* of porn.' She shuts the laptop and rests it on the table. 'So, do you want to head there?'

Shepherd looks at me, arms folded, eyes narrowed. 'I think we need hard evidence before—'

'Luke, Luke, Luke.' I clap the big sod on the arm. 'Remember that I outrank you here.'

'So?'

'So I can just raid this place any time I want.'

'I don't report to you. And you're going nowhere

without Ally's approval.'

'Oh, you're going running to Daddy, are you? Boo hoo.'

Shepherd unfolds his arms, fists clenched tight like he's going to lamp us. Good to get a reaction out of the prick for once, instead of him standing there like a lump of granite. 'Get over yourself.'

'Luke, we need to get in there and find Falconer. His smack is killing people. Heard that one of those lassies your boys took to the hospital popped her clogs. Could be he's buggered off, knowing his heroin's catching up with him. We found *three* passports in his locker. Maybe he's got another. Maybe he's in the wind too, like Drake.'

Hunter grabs Shepherd's arm and pushes him away. Didn't see him even entering the room! Christ! 'Guys, you look like you're going to tear lumps out of each other.'

I give Shepherd a big grin. 'Saved you there, big boy.'

Oh, he wants to smack us into next week. I love winding that prick up. But he turns to Hunter. 'What's up, Craig?'

'I know Kenny Falconer.'

I frown at him. 'How well?'

'Pretty well. He was in my brother's year at school. Porty High. Think his parents split up and he moved to Wester Hailes with his mum. He's a nasty wee shite.'

'You ever speak to him much?'

Hunter nodded slowly. 'Could say that. He was a bully.' He shut his eyes. 'He was responsible for a mate's suicide.'

'He's older than you?'

'A year younger, but he was kept back a year. Bullied the shite out of my mate...' Doesn't name him, does he? Weird. 'Angus killed himself. Jumped in front of a train.'

'Sorry to hear that.' Am I hell. This boy having a personal beef against Falconer is golden. I can use him as a weapon. Get him all riled up and ready to kill. 'So, do you think we should pay him a visit now or later?'

'We need to hit him hard. Kenny will run.'

The door opens and Christ, it's getting crowded in here. 'Boys. And girl.' It's James Anderson. Christ, the Leith Walk gang don't know they're born having this fanny-mouthed arsehole as a SOCO. 'Running a million things just now, but I've got some good news. The blood toxicology came back, and the two women in hospital were on the same heroin that you found in that locker.'

'Nailed.'

Anderson steps aside and scowls at someone. 'Didn't see you there.'

Cullen's lurking out there like a wee goblin. A very pretty one, mind. But still a goblin. 'Just been down at the PM and Deeley's confirmed it from the victim's blood.' He hands Shepherd something. 'Anyway, here's the warrant.'

'Thanks.' He pockets it without us checking it.

I give Shepherd the biggest grin. 'Where's the warrant for?'

'It's for another case.' But he's blushing. Sneaky bastard. That warrant we used at the gym was phoney. 'So, I think Hunter's correct. We hit Falconer now. Visit the bookshop, see if he's there.'

Shepherd has his phone open but his sugar daddy clearly isn't saving him this time. 'Okay.'

'Excellent.' I crack my knuckles but it's a soft clip rather than a mean-sounding pop. 'Okay, so DC Jain, DC Hunter and DS Shepherd, let's get around there.'

That Cullen boy folds his arms. 'You don't need me?'

'I'll get uniform back-up, sunshine. You can get along to the Xmas party.'

'Right.' Boy does he look pissed off. Mouth hanging open, eyes drooping. Still, he doesn't moan and that's got to count for something.

I don't need some daft wee Acting DC making an arse of things. But you never know where these boys will end up. Probably back in uniform, but you just never know, so I clap him on the arm. 'Imagine how much sweeter that eggnog will taste without having to do a dunt, sunshine. See you in the morning.'

'Tomorrow's Saturday. And I'm off.'

15

Cullen

Trouble with arriving late was Cullen had missed the food and the best of the drink.

He stood in the middle of the function room and just wanted to get out of there.

Forty, maybe fifty officers sat around drinking, with another twenty or so strutting their stuff to *Oh, What A Night*, though Cullen thought it might be called *December 1963*. Either way, the dancing was rancid.

Christmas parties in uniform were usually a few pints in a pub in Bathgate, then a boozy Italian or a very boozy curry. And the hardcore alcoholics wouldn't be out — they'd be stuck at home with their supermarket whiskies, hiding their addiction from the brass, who all knew anyway.

But here, the function room was filled with buffet food and buffet booze.

And DC Paul 'Elvis' Gordon wasn't hiding his alcoholism. His sideburns almost touched his jawline, and he embraced the shape and hairstyle of Vegas-era Elvis. In his left hand, a glass of thick red wine filled to the brim. In his right, two champagne flutes, though the sparkle had long since faded. And somehow he was chomping on a sausage roll. He half-finished chewing and swallowed it down with a drink of fizz, his backwash depositing pastry crumbs in the glass. And spilled the second flute down his shirt. 'Ah, bollocks.' Puff pastry spat out, landing at Cullen's feet.

'Evening, Paul.' Cullen reached for a glass of red from a side table filled with them and inspected it for signs it had been tampered with. Fingerprints or lipstick marks. Seemed clean, so he sipped it and savoured the balsamic vinegar tang.

'Look like a SOCO there, Scott.' Elvis was focusing on a space about a metre to the right of Cullen, presumably where the second version he was seeing was currently standing, though Elvis's shifting gaze made him out to be a moving target. 'Examining it for evidence, eh?' He laughed, then tried to drink his empty champagne glass. And succeeded in spilling red wine straight onto the floor.

Aye, Elvis was going to need a wee help home tonight. Again.

Cullen grabbed his arm and led him over to a table out of the glare of the high heid yins, who were sitting over by the speakers. Cullen settled Elvis down and placed the wine glass just out of his reach, still amazingly half full.

Some doowop scat burst out of the speakers. The opening to *Come On, Eileen*.

Cullen groaned.

Elvis jabbed a finger at a Cullen somewhere to his left. 'Tell you, Scott. This is an absolute banger of a tune.' He frowned and stared right at Cullen. 'Dexys are a heavily underrated band.'

'Take your word for it.' Cullen sank a good chunk of his wine and started to feel that glow. 'The plonk's not too bad.'

'Aye, only drinking that because the beer was so shite here. I mean, rank lagers all along the bar and not even a Guinness safety pint. It's 2010, but the beer here is like it's from the fifties. Red pish. Or *lager.*' Elvis reached over for his wine and managed to claw it on the fourth attempt. But he took great care in sliding it over, then lowered his head and sucked at the wine.

Cullen was nowhere near drunk enough to put up

with that kind of nonsense. 'Think you've had enough, Paul.'

'Had nowhere near enough, mate.' Elvis ran a hand across his lips. 'You missed Big Jim Turnbull's speech earlier.'

'Aye, well. Small mercies, eh?'

Elvis tugged at Cullen's cheek, the correct Cullen this time. 'Where you been?'

'Out and about.'

'Where?'

'Not getting in on the raid on the bookshop.'

'Aw, diddums.' Elvis cackled, then sipped more wine. 'You know your problem, Scott? Too keen. Way too keen. You're waaaaaaay too keen. Waaaaaaaaaaaaaaaaaaay too.' Burp. 'Keen.'

The absolute best thing about drunks was how much unsolicited advice you got from them. Buggers could solve world hunger from the bottom of a wine glass.

The dance floor had settled into late wedding dancing, with a scrum tackling the song's breakdown section where it slowed right down. Cullen couldn't watch them speed up to a mad frenzy. 'Too keen. That right, aye?'

'Aye, completely. You want my advice, you should just get your head low, and let things happen to you.'

'Like you do?'

'Aye! I mean, I'm going places, Scott. Changed days.'

Elvis swung his finger around the room. 'Too many of these cops are old school. Speaking to people, all that crap. The future, my friend, the future is in computers.' He tapped his nose like he'd just been given the secrets of the universe. 'Mark my words.'

'Give me an example.'

That floored Elvis. Literally. He slid off his chair.

Cullen had to help him back up. Big lump was in danger of hauling him down with him. 'You should get home, Elvis.'

'Quit it, I'm fine.' He brushed away Cullen's helping hand and sat in his chair again. 'Totally fine.'

Cullen took a sip of his wine and scanned the rest of the tables for anyone less shit-faced than Elvis. Part of him wanted to get smashed, but the senior officers table was like a panopticon in reverse, with each one scanning the room for dafties taking it too far.

And at least two of them had clocked Elvis as Daftie numero uno.

Cullen pulled out his phone and texted a local cabbie who'd given him a bit of info recently:

Got a fare for you, Bongo. Southside to Broxburn

Cullen put his phone away just as it chimed with a new message:

How likely to spew?

Cullen checked Elvis again. Truth was, maybe eighty percent likely. Then again, Elvis was always the last man standing on nights out. That kind of invincibility meant vomit was rare.

Not quite sober as a judge, but he won't be sick

Buzz.

Thirty quid. Another fifty if he chucks

Cullen texted Elvis's address, adding:

Soon as you can, Bongo. And I owe you. Text me when you're outside

Elvis tossed his wine back and was looking around for more. 'Trick I've been pulling is doing IT stuff for people. Hoover up all that work, become a specialist.' He ran a hand across his lips. 'Take it all on. Become an *expert*. I'll be indispensable.'

'You'll be pigeonholed.'

'I'll be what?'

'You'll get saddled with all that shite, Paul.'

'Nah, nah, nah. You don't know what you're talking

about.' Elvis sipped more wine. 'Here's the thing. This case you and Hunter are working with Big Luke. Pair of fannies can't track down that Becky lassie who skipped out on the court appearance. Well.' He tapped his nose. 'Let's just say I'll get a result before you two do.'

'Pleased to hear it. Tell me, how will you manage it?'

'Not spilling.' But he did. His glass hit the table. Lucky for Elvis, it was empty.

Cullen righted the glass, which was much easier than righting Elvis. He was like a dead weight in his arms. 'Okay, Paul. Let's get you some fresh air.' He marched him out of the door on the darkest side of the function room. He hoped none of the bosses had seen them, but you just never knew. Cops spotted things most people didn't.

The cold air hit his cheeks like a slap from a spurned lover. And Cullen would know. His phone thrummed in his pockets and he looked around the car park.

A black cab was idling by the entrance. The back door opened and DC Yvonne Flockhart stepped out, dressed for a wedding rather than a police piss-up. Tall and raven-haired, and with that knowing smile on her face. 'Evening, Scott.' She reached through the window and handed over some money, then looked at Elvis, then Cullen. 'Christ, Scott. What's happened?'

'He's just feeling a bit under the weather, that's all.'

'Under the wine, more like.' She grabbed Elvis's arm and helped Cullen lead him away from danger.

'Don't want to go.' Elvis was looking at Yvonne. 'Please, Scott. I'll behave. Promise!'

Aye, like shite you will.

Cullen leaned low and there was Bongo behind the wheel, eyes narrowed with suspicion. He opened the door and held the back one for Elvis to clamber inside.

'No way is that boy safe.' Bongo was shaking his head, as many wobbles on his shaved head as on his jowls. 'Eighty quid, up front.'

Christ.

Cullen opened his wallet and forked out the money. 'I want the fifty back if he doesn't spew.'

'Oh, he's going to.' Bongo folded the money and pocketed it. 'Absolute pain in the arse if I have to clean the cab, man. You've no idea. It gets *everywhere*.' He got back in with a loud slam and drove off, spraying pebbles at Cullen.

Yvonne watched the car slide out of the parking area, weaving around the stone circle in the middle of the drive. 'Well, Elvis has left the building.'

'That was a wee while ago.' Cullen smiled at her. 'You missed the meal too?'

'Don't mention it.' She shook her head. 'Absolutely starving.'

'Me too.'

'Come on, I smell sausage rolls.' Yvonne charged inside and eased her coat off by the cloakroom, not that it was attended. 'Last days of Rome in here.'

'Aye, I doubt Elvis will be the last victim of tonight's excesses.' Cullen checked the dance floor, now thumping with that Killers song, and at least twice as busy as the last one. The bosses' table was empty. 'Christ, you've not lived until you've seen Ally Davenport dancing to *Mr Brightside*.'

Yvonne laughed. 'Where's the wine?'

Cullen led her over to the booze table, which was further depleted since the last time he'd visited. 'Red or white?'

'Both.' She grabbed a glass of each.

Cullen took another red and led her to the table where he'd babysat Elvis. His glass seemed untouched since his escape, but he couldn't trust someone like Malky McKeown not to spike it or just do something vile to it. 'So, what kept you back?'

Yvonne sank half of her white in one go. 'Young Becky.'

Cullen winced. 'Elvis was muttering something about it.'

'Tell you, he better produce a hail Mary from out of his pocket, because we are nowhere, Scott. I've been chasing down leads all day on it, thanks to you and Craig dropping a bollock on it.'

'Hardly dropped a bollock.' Cullen caught a flash of driving to the hospital, the now-dead wife of Happy Jack on the back seat. Alive. 'We got sidelined with something else. Think you'll find Becky?'

'Hardly. It's like she's just vanished.'

'Like the suspect. Flying to Argentina as we speak.' Cullen sipped the wine and let the peppery tang nibble his tongue, then waved his hand around the room. 'And we have no choice but to sit in a cheap function room, dancing to *Don't Stop Believing.*'

On the dance floor, Davenport was back-to-back with DCI Turnbull, screaming into air microphones.

'That was your case this morning.' There went the last of Yvonne's white. 'You should feel bad for us having to do your dirty work.'

'Well, nature of the beast.'

'Craig said you saved two lives?'

'Something like that.'

'You did, or you didn't?'

'Two were okay, or at least okay enough for the paramedics to sort out.' Cullen took a big dent out of his glass. 'I drove the other two up to the ERI, jumping all the red lights.' He swallowed down bile. 'One didn't make it. Ally was at her PM an hour ago. Thought we'd saved her.'

'That must be hard.'

'*So* hard.'

Yvonne pulled her gaze away from Cullen's long enough to search the room. 'Thought Craig would be here.'

Cullen finished his first glass. 'He got taken on a raid by this idiot DI based at Leith Walk.'

'Right.' She finished her glass now. 'Could've told me.'

Cullen didn't want to get stuck between two quarrelling lovers, but she looked like she needed to talk. 'You okay?'

'Not really.' She took a big drink of red now. 'Craig's... Well, he's Craig.'

'Tell me about it.'

She glared at him. 'What, are you saying "tell me about it" like you actually want me to? Or you want me to shut up?'

'Either. If you want to talk, I'll listen.'

She sat back and let out a big sigh. 'Things are difficult between us. Have been for a while. Craig... He's always hiding stuff from me, makes it really bloody hard to know what to do about anything.'

'What kind of thing?'

'Little things. He thinks I don't notice, but...' Another glug of wine. 'I love him, right, but I'm just not sure he loves me.'

'I know he does.'

She winced. 'Well, maybe we're just not suited. Or

this isn't the right time for us.'

'That could be the case.'

'Mm.' She stared into her glass.

Cullen leaned forward. 'This morning, when we were looking for Becky, Shepherd said something like "That makes sense". Craig was standing in this trance, just after he saw Happy Jack. Any idea what he meant?'

Yvonne nodded. 'I mean, they served together.'

'I know, but... Craig froze when he saw him. Just stood there. Like, worse than Elvis was. And he was sober.'

'Right.' She sighed, and her shoulders dropped. 'You know he's got PTSD?'

'I didn't, no.' It explained a lot. A hell of a lot. 'This what he's been keeping from you?'

'Partly. But... It's complex. He should be on medication or getting counselling or both. But he's in denial about the whole thing. Thinks he'll get sacked if he talks to anyone about it.'

'So he covers it up?'

'Tries to. But clearly Luke knows what's going on.'

'Right. Which means half the brass do.' Cullen waved over at the dance floor. Davenport was taking all the Kirsty McColl lines in that Pogues song, shouting them at Turnbull. Seemed very cathartic calling him a "cheap, lousy faggot". He looked back at Yvonne. 'I want to help.'

'Me or Craig?'

'Both. Either.'

'Well, Craig is the one who needs to get help. What he's been through has broken him. Or maybe that's too harsh. Damaged him. But either way, he needs help.'

'And you?'

'It's driving me crazy, Scott. I love Craig, but I can't keep doing this. Someone acting the way he does, you can only do it for so long before it eats you up. And he's talking about having kids.'

'I see. How do you feel about that?'

'I mean, I want them at some point, right? We're still young. But I just don't think Craig will ever be ready. What if he has a PTSD flashback when he's cradling our baby?'

'Aye, I see that. Must be tough.'

'You have no idea. Single guys like you, Scott, you've got it easy.' She finished her glass and reached across the table for a bottle sitting in the shadow, then frowned at it. 'This has barely been touched.' She leaned over and topped up Cullen's glass with Chateauneuf-du-Prestonpans, then filled hers to the brim, just like Elvis had.

'Cheers.' Cullen reached behind him and found another barely drunk bottle. 'So, about Craig. What can I do to help?'

16

Hunter

The traffic filled both sides of Gorgie Road, stuck at both ends by the grinding drills of yet another set of Christmas roadworks. Some bastard in the council was determined to piss off as many of west Edinburgh's denizens as they could. The stink of tar mixed with roasting meat from the burger van serving up a late tea to the workers on the night shift.

Made Hunter feel sick, hauling him back to somewhere he didn't want to go. Somewhere hot, underground. The same smells, just a different source.

The sign for Boab's Books caught the latest gust of wind and made that squealing sound again. The shop was as battered looking as the sign. Grimy windows that didn't clearly show what kind of shop it was, or even if it actually sold books.

Hunter didn't know any of the characters, their in-jokes, the longstanding beefs, who to trust, who to avoid.

Actually, he knew Chantal Jain. She knew what she was doing, but this wasn't her rodeo and she stood down the street on the phone, presumably to her boss.

But Hunter knew he needed to avoid DI Bain. That was clear. Guy was an arsehole. And more than just a little dangerous. He'd seen his type before.

'Here, Shaz, can you pull your finger out and get uniform to pull their collective fingers out, aye?' Bain laughed. 'Unless they've got whole hands up there?'

DS McNeill gave a warm smile, way kinder than he or his joke deserved. Showed real character to be treated like shite and to not buckle under it. Then again, it was 2010 and people like Bain shouldn't be in charge of anything other than a drawer full of paper-clips. 'Right, sir, I'll see what's what.'

Hunter shuffled over to stand next to Shepherd, lurking at the periphery and smiling like he'd at least read up on this show before he'd been asked to participate. 'You know them?'

'A few of them, aye.' Shepherd folded his arms that bit tighter. 'Bain is... Well.' He shook his head, but was grimacing rather than grinning. 'He's Bain. Sharon's a good cop. She used to be in my team, way before you.'

'Right.' Hunter watched her bark out orders to a beaten-down clown in a uniform, just missing the giant shoes and the lapel flower spraying water. 'What's the story with her and Bain?'

'No story, Craig. Just mentor-mentee.'

'Well, it seems to me like he's bullying her.'

'Some people need coaxing.'

'How?'

'Sharon has a bit of a lazy streak. Don't get me wrong, you give her something she cares about, there's not a cop alive who'll do it better, and few dead ones. But try getting her to do something she doesn't like? Forget it.'

'Sounds like Cullen.'

Shepherd grinned. 'Peas in a pod, them two.'

Hunter shivered as another blast of the arctic wind hit them. 'Missing the party?'

'Watching a load of arseholes boogying to *Brown Eyed Girl*? Not for me, Clive.'

Hunter frowned at him. 'Clive?'

'Relax, Craig. It's a football joke, not a new nickname.'

'That's a relief.'

McNeill charged back towards them from their post

by the chemist, and nodded at Bain. 'They're good to go, sir. Back entrance secure.'

'Bloody better be.' Bain stared along the road for a few seconds, his moustache twitching, then focused on Hunter. 'Right, Big Yin, you and DS McNeill here are to form my vanguard.'

'Your what?'

Bain rolled his eyes. 'You're going in first, you big daftie.' He shook his head, but was very definitely grinning. 'Me and Luke will lurk around here, make sure you two do your job. Capiche?'

'Got it.' Hunter gazed at McNeill, just in time to catch a flicker of a smirk. 'Ready when you are, Sarge.'

'No time like the present.' McNeill clicked her right finger just in time for the nearby traffic lights to change to red, then charged across the road.

Hunter had to jog to catch up, checking he had his baton and cuffs readily accessible. His pepper spray was in his pocket, but deep enough that it wouldn't go off accidentally in his own face.

McNeill looked back across the road, got a nod, then gave one to Hunter. 'You first.'

'Sarge.' Hunter entered the shop. The bell gave a broken tinkle.

The place was crammed full of bookshelves and a ghost of cigarette smoke, though the air didn't have that telltale blue tinge. Maybe most of the stock came from smoking homes. Or the tired-looking bookseller behind the till had just sucked on five fags out the back door and left it open.

Hunter took charge and walked up to the till. 'Nice evening.'

'Is it?' She looked him up and down, then sipped from a white mug emblazoned with "Aye, darlin'" and no clues as to what that was referencing. If anything. 'I'm just about to shut, so if you want to grab something, I can still put it through the till.'

Hunter leaned on the table. 'Looking for Kenny.'

'Kenny who?'

'Falconer.' Hunter opened his warrant card and flashed it to her. 'Police. Just need a word with him.'

Another sip of coffee. 'He's not here.'

'Seen him recently?'

'Not for a while, why?'

The door gave its broken tinkle again. Bain stepped in, hands in pockets, whistling away.

Hunter focused on the cashier again. 'Are you in charge here?'

'No.'

'Who is then?'

'Ricky.' She thumbed over at a set of stairs between two bookcases. 'He's up in the flat.'

Bain stepped between McNeill and Hunter. 'Shaz,

you stay here. Me and the Big Yin will see what's what.' He clapped Hunter's arm then skipped off up the stairs.

Hunter followed, but clutched his baton. 'You got a warrant for this?'

'Warrant schmarrant.' Bain stopped at the top and rapped his knuckles on the door. 'Ricky? Police!'

Hunter stared hard at Bain. 'I'm a bit uncomfortable about—'

'Son, you're a constable. I'm an inspector. Ergo, this is my neck on the line. You follow my lead, capiche?'

Aye, and Hunter had never been prodded with the big shitty stick of blame, had he? 'You keep saying "capiche", but it doesn't make you look bad ass.'

'Rightio.' Bain smirked as he hit the door again. 'Ricky?' He paused for a few seconds, then pressed his ear to the door. 'Can you hear that?'

Hunter took his place at the door and listened hard. Sounded like a series of dull thuds. 'Someone opening a window?'

'My thinking exactly.' Bain tapped the door with his shoe. 'Open sesame.'

Another joy of being the lowest rung on the ladder. Well, except for Cullen but he wasn't here.

Then another thud and a scream, 'Ah, you bastard!'

'Come on, Craig!'

Hunter stepped back and took his aim. 'This is on

you.' He took a step back and charged the door, knee up, drove his boots into the door next to the latch.

Wood splintered as he crashed through, sending the door trim halfway cross the room as the door banged backwards on its protesting hinges.

Over by the window, a bony arse was poking out of the gap, skinny legs in skinny jeans kicking against the air, the window pane pinning his waist down.

Bain stayed in the doorway.

Hunter raced over and hauled the window up with a tearing shriek, not all of which came from the body belonging to the arse he was pulling back into the room.

A man in his twenties. A Wu Tang hoodie about six Xs too big for him and faded jeans four inches too small. Giant white basketball shoes, looking box fresh.

Hunter pushed him against the wall nearest the window. 'Ricky?'

Stoned eyes looked up at him, but didn't really focus on anything. 'Depends who's asking.'

'Police, son.' Bain joined them by the window and peered out onto Gorgie Road. 'Got a few of our pals out there, you know. If you'd got out of here and hadn't buggered your ankle when you landed, you'd have been nicked.' He waved out of the window. 'Evening, boys.' Then he turned to face Ricky. 'As it is, I can just pretend you getting stuck in the window was a sex game.'

'Shut up, man.'

Bain smiled. 'You got any way of proving you're Ricky and not Kenny Falconer?'

'Eh?'

'Son, I need a driver's license or a passport.'

'Right. Let me get you one.'

Hunter checked with Bain, got a nod, then let Ricky go from his position by the window.

Ricky dusted himself off, then grabbed an over-stuffed wallet from the table in front of a games console. He pulled out a driver's license and held it out for Hunter. 'See?'

Hunter snapped on a glove and inspected it. 'Richard Duncan Falconer. Date of birth, fourth of November, 1986.'

'Christ, you must've had a tough childhood.' Bain bellowed with laughter. 'Grow up in Gotham or something?'

Ricky laughed. 'You're hardly Batman.'

'More like Commissioner Gordon.' Bain snatched the card out of Hunter's grip, then inspected it like a jeweller at a rare diamond. 'It's probably real, this. Or a very good fake.'

'It's real!'

Hunter spotted some paperwork near to where the wallet had been. He shuffled over and checked it. A red passport wrapped around some prints. Richard Duncan

Falconer. He unfolded the paperwork. Bingo. 'Sir, these are plane tickets to Buenos Aires.' Sitting on top of a blister pack of diazepam, half empty but still enough to get the worst flyer in the world through even the longest haul.

Bain leaned in close to Ricky. 'What's in Buenos Aires?'

'Going to the football!'

'Football? You a big River Plate fan, or something?'

'Los Millonarios? Hardly.' Ricky gave a slack-jawed laugh. 'Boca Juniors, all the way.'

'Huh.' Bain smoothed down his moustache. 'Where's the flight from, Craig?'

Hunter checked again. 'Newcastle, sir. Tomorrow at twelve.'

'Weird thing.' Bain stepped closer to Ricky. No physical contact, but the way he handled himself... It gave even Hunter the creeps. 'Because we lost a dirty wee raping bastard. He was on the plane from Newcastle to Buenos Aires. But he went today.'

'Don't know anything about it.'

'You don't know an Alexander Drake?'

Ricky shrugged.

'Where's your brother, Ricky?'

'What brother?'

Bain sighed. 'Do I have to keep repeating myself?' He drilled his gaze into Ricky's eyes. 'Where's Kenny?'

Ricky looked away. 'No idea.'

'You meeting him in Buenos Aires?'

'Where's that?'

'Where your plane tickets are for, you numpty!'

'Doubt it.'

'So where is he?'

'God knows.'

Bain stood there for a few seconds, silently fuming. Then he looked over at Hunter. 'Take this prick down the station, Craig.'

17

Cullen

A taxi whizzed past them, slooshing through the rain and spraying the puddle in their direction, but just missing.

Another had its yellow light on and slowed to see if they wanted in, if they wanted shielding from the driving rain.

Cullen waved him away. 'Guess it's true what they say.' He struggled to put one foot anywhere near the other. If he wasn't clinging on to Yvonne, he'd go down like a sack of tatties. 'Don't eat on an empty stomach.'

'You mean don't drink on an empty stomach.' Yvonne was slurring her speech. 'Right?'

Cullen stopped but it felt like his head was still walking. 'What did I say?'

'Don't eat on one.'

'Right. Well, obviously that's good advice.' He blinked hard a few times and tried to get his bearings. Jamie's pub. That meant Causewayside. 'Where is it you live again?'

'Grange Loan.' She waved ahead of them. 'Not far now.' He felt her hand tighten around his. 'I've heard stories about you, Scott.'

Cullen stopped and let her hand go. The street spun around his head. 'What kind of stories?'

'About how you're a ladies' man, as my dad would say. How I should be worried about you and your reputation. How you're a bit of a shagger.'

'I'm not.' Cullen wanted to burp but was afraid what would come up. Stale wine and stomach acid wasn't a nice cocktail, especially served on a pavement. 'Who told you?'

'This nurse?'

That explained it. Christ. She was making his life an absolute hell.

Well, not that bad. But still...

'I was at the hospital today, speaking to the people who treated Becky when she... She asked if I worked with you. And... Aye. Told me you're shagging your way around the place.'

Bollocks to it. She deserved the truth. 'The thing is, I kissed her. That's true. But she's not someone I want to be with. That's it. So I didn't see her again. And it seemed fine, but... But I had this thing with a doctor at the hospital.'

'And this nurse got jealous and started spreading rumours?'

'Aye. I'm serious.' Cullen felt that sting in his nostrils that signified tears were on the way. He sucked in a deep breath through them, trying to get them under control. 'I don't want to sound like an arrogant prick, even though I am. But that's what happened. And I think I really like this doctor.'

'Yule?'

Cullen nodded. 'You know her?'

'I can see why you'd be into her.'

'I'm sick of being single. I want to share my life with someone.' Cullen looked away from her. A night bus hurtled past, heading for Dalkeith and its Midlothian cousins. 'I've got a reputation for being a moaner, why I've not got a tenure, all this. But there's a good reason why I'm a cop, why I push myself to be the best cop I can. And it's complex. Or complicated.'

'You want to talk about it?'

Cullen shrugged. 'And it's connected to the trouble I have with relationships and... And it's... all so complicated.'

Across the street, a gang of students were larking around. Maybe stayed in Pollock Halls over by the Park, or maybe a flat near here. Either way, they were up to malarkey.

'We're here.' Yvonne waved up at a standard Edinburgh tenement. The street had a few of them at the start then gave way to posher houses. 'My flat.'

'I should go.'

'You want to come in for a chat?'

'I really don't know, Yvonne.'

Yvonne unlocked the stairwell door and didn't look at him. 'Because of Craig?'

Cullen shrugged. 'Because I need to get to bed. I've got a busy day tomorrow.'

'You can just say hi to Craig. It'll be fine. You look like you really need to talk to someone. And I'm actually a pretty good listener.'

Cullen sighed, his breath misting in the cold night air. 'It's not just that. Sometimes the booze makes me feel sad and introspective. This is one of those nights. I should walk it off.'

'You live in Portobello, though.'

'It's fine. About an hour from here.'

'I understand... that need, Scott.' She slowly ran a hand down her face. 'But you're all about beating yourself up. Whatever's happened, you can talk to me about it.'

Cullen looked up at the flat. No sign Craig was actually in. And Christ, he really did want to talk to someone. Professionally seemed a bit too much just now, like he was taking himself too seriously. But a friend offering an ear?

He could make sure she got up the stairs.

Sod it, he should take her up on it.

'Aye, go on.'

'Good lad.' She opened the door wide and staggered in. The stairwell was filled with student bikes all locked to the banister, and smelled of Christmas Party perfume. A fat little tortie hissed at them, then scurried up the stairs.

Yvonne followed it up. She didn't look like she could stay upright for very long. Lucky for her, Cullen was behind her, close enough to catch her, but her arse was almost in his face.

Cullen kept a tight grip on the varnished wood as he winched himself up.

Yvonne sprayed her keys on the marble floor. 'Buggery bollocks.' She crouched down to grab them but the crouch became a sit pretty quickly. She yawned into her fist. 'Christ, I'm so bloody tired.'

'Long shifts just now, eh?' Cullen reached out a hand for her and hauled her up. And went flying backwards into their door.

Yvonne giggled like a schoolgirl. 'Oh my god, Scott. I

might die.' She stood and unfurled her keys, then opened the lock at the third go. 'Craig?' Her bellow rang around the stairwell more than the flat. 'You home?'

Cullen had to lean against the doorframe. 'I should go.'

'Scott, it feels like there's something you want to talk about.'

'I'm not hitting on you, Yvonne.'

'I know you're not. I want to listen.'

'Because of Craig.'

'Mm, but you're talking to me.' She stepped inside and tossed her keys on the table. They slid to the floor. 'I need to pee. Get me something to drink.'

'Sure thing.' Cullen walked down the hallway and found the kitchen. Basically, half of the living room.

So. Drink. Booze was a very bad idea. Tea or coffee, then.

He filled the kettle from the overly complicated tap and tried to find the button to set it to boil. There. At least it was rattling quickly.

No sign of a bean grinder or even a cafetière, but he found a serviceable tub of instant. One of those fair trade ones that actually tasted like coffee rather than the ashes of a loved one.

Christ, he needed to sober up and fast.

No, he needed to go. He took out his phone, but it wasn't in that pocket.

Bollocks. Shite, shite, shite.

He found it in his jacket. A missed call and sixteen texts from Bongo. He scanned them, basically dog's abuse for Elvis vomiting in the back of the cab. And Cullen would never see that eighty quid again.

He texted:

Any chance of a trip home?

Cullen found the mugs in a cupboard. Some romantic ones with lovey-dovey slogans that were all chipped. He left them in favour of some plain IKEA jobs, tipping in spoonfuls of instant, then pouring hot water just before the boil.

Buzz.

Bugger off

Crap. He'd pissed Bongo off big time. And that's why you don't mix business with pleasure. He needed Bongo's info way more than Elvis needed a lift home. And now he needed to keep him onside.

Seriously, mate. Desperate here. Twenty quid

He rummaged in the fridge for milk, but just found some oat-based stuff.

He shouldn't be here. Not in this state. Craig was the kind to jump to conclusions. And that weird PTSD flashback stuff, well; Cullen had seen the upshot of that, getting pushed back onto the sand. His bum still hurt. That bone at the back. The cock six? Still sore, despite the medicinal booze.

Buzz.

No chance before 12. Still cleaning out the cab

Ill take that

But typing "cheers" on a numeric keyboard was beyond Cullen, so he just sent it.

Just over an hour. Good.

Yvonne stumbled in and sat on the sofa, yawning into her fist. 'Coffee. Mm.'

'No milk.'

'Use Craig's oat milk.'

'Will do.' Cullen tipped oat milk into the mugs. Hopefully it didn't taste rank. He grabbed the handles and staggered over.

First problem, there was only the sofa, so he had to sit next to her.

Second, Yvonne had a bottle of Sambuca open and was pouring two shots.

Oh shite.

18

Hunter

The interview room was deadly silent, save for the clock hanging squint on the wall. The emptiness seemed to make the ticking louder, like someone was hitting drums at a metronomic beat.

Hunter sat forward and waved a hand across Ricky's face.

No reaction.

Just the same glaikit expression on his face. Mouth hanging open, drool encrusted around his lips. Eyes staring at a spot halfway between the middle of the table and heaven.

Bain huffed out a big sigh. 'Well, screw me six ways

to Sunday. Don't even need the Duty Doctor in here, do we? This boy's off his coupon on that Valium.'

Hunter couldn't disagree with the diagnosis, as unprofessionally as it was given. 'Must've taken half the packet before we got there. Make sure he was chilled by the time he arrived at Newcastle tomorrow morning. Or if you're going to jail, you don't got there sober.'

Bain pinched his nose and shut his eyes, mercifully silent for a few seconds. 'Probably why he got his arse stuck in that window.'

'We probably saved his life, sir. You should still get the Duty Doctor in here. Those pills are deadly.'

'Know a thing about them, aye?'

'Back in my army days, aye. Couple of the lads weren't the best flyers, as you can imagine. And a military transport doesn't have a Spider-Man film playing on the back of the seat in front of you, does it? So they popped a couple of Valium.'

'You boys.' Bain stood up and prodded his fingers off the screen of a phone that looked like it had beamed in from the set of *Star Trek*. 'My ex-wife used to take one of them when we flew to Florida with the boy for our summer break. Spaced her out for days, I tell you. But if this arsehole scranned half the packet? Game's a bogie, Craig. Christ, we should've spoken to him back at his flat while he was still on the same planee of existence as us.' He huffed out a deep sigh, whistling around his moustache. 'Fine. I'll deal with this. You get to this Christmas party. I'd say let your hair down, but there's none of it.' He reached over and scratched at Hunter's stubble.

Hunter stepped away from the seedy bastard and checked the clock. Midnight, already. And he could only imagine the state of some of them. Cullen and free wine. *Elvis*. Christ. And maybe Yvonne was already on the Sambuca. A day off tomorrow so she'd be hitting it hard. 'Not really in the mood for a party.'

'Want a lift home?'

'I'm fine. The walk will do me good. It's just up the road. So, you need me for the interview first thing?'

'On a Saturday?'

'I can come in.'

'Cheeky bit of OT?'

'I'll take Time Off In Lieu. Just want to find Falconer.'

'Personal between you, aye?'

'Aye.'

'Okay. Well, you get in here first thing and we'll see if this boy's back on the same planet as us.'

Hunter zipped up his jacket. In no way was he on the same planet as Brian Bain. Not even the same solar system.

19

Cullen

Cullen rested the fresh cups and slumped down next to her, trying to keep as far away as possible.

What the hell was he doing here?

'So, Scott. Talk to me.'

He nodded. But he didn't look at her. Or the Sambuca.

'But first, let's toast us.' She handed him his shot glass.

'Us?'

'Us being pals. That's all.' She stared hard at him as she downed the shot. Those dark eyes, full of mischief and mystery. Her hair draped over one shoulder. Bare arms. And her top was a bit lower, wasn't it?

Cullen should just walk out. Sod Bongo, he should flag down a cab, then get some sleep and revel in the brutal hangover. It'd be all over.

But something kept him there, stopped him leaving.

'Sod it.' He necked the shot and a blast of aniseed filled his mouth. 'Christ, that's rank.'

'It's good for you, though.' She topped up both glasses and put a hand on his knee. 'Now. About you being a shagger.'

'I'm not.'

'Look, whatever. Sex can be an addiction, just like drinking, gambling or whatever. At the root of it all, you're fending off death. Inch by inch.'

'This sounds a bit deep.'

'Because it is, Scott.'

'I didn't know you were a psychologist.'

'I did a degree in it.'

Shite.

'Most of the time, I feel fine. Work helps. But when a woman shows the slightest flicker of interest, I'm like a greyhound after a hare. And afterwards... I'm filled with so much revulsion.' Saying it out loud felt good, like he was three stone lighter. Or floating in space.

'Why do you think you have sex with so many women?'

Cullen let out a long, slow sigh. 'I don't know.'

'But you do have sex with a lot?'

'Not a *lot* lot, but... some?'

'Those nurses?'

'Nope.'

'The paramedic?'

'God no.'

'That doctor?'

'Right, aye.'

She put the fresh glass in his hand. 'Drink up.'

Cullen slung it back without any hesitation. The spirit burnt through the wine and he felt a warm tingle in his gut.

And it was melting in here. Like forty degrees or something.

Craig always liked it hot in the car, stood to reason he'd like it hot in the flat.

Cullen shrugged off his jacket and reached for his coffee. Way too hot to drink.

Yvonne put another shot in his hands, then necked her own. She pursed her lips. 'Outside, you said it's all connected. To what?'

'I don't know.'

'You don't have to talk to me, Scott, but it might help if you told someone what's going on?'

Cullen cradled his coffee mug. Almost cool enough to consider drinking.

Something in him made him want to open up to her. And it wasn't just the booze. He couldn't pick out what it was.

Christ, maybe she was flirting with him, but there was this electricity between them. Always had been.

And he was dicking about with Helen Yule. He liked her, of course he did, but it was more what she represented. Maturity. Stability. A future. As much as what she reminded him of, what he was trying to conquer.

Maybe Yvonne wanted that too.

So why was he in her flat, when his mate—her boyfriend—wasn't?

Because she was a friend and wanted to help. Focus on that.

'Something happened to me when I was a kid.'

Yvonne frowned. 'What, you were bullied?'

'God no.'

'Abused?'

'Aye.'

'Beaten?'

'No.'

'Was it sexual?'

'Umm.'

'Were they older?'

'No...'

'Scott, the offer's there.'

Cullen necked the shot and felt it all bubbling

around in his guts. The wine, the Sambuca, the disgusting truth.

'What happened? Did he rape you?'

'Not all abuse is done by men.' Cullen tightened his grip on the handle. 'It was a teacher. My English teacher. Miss Carnegie. She was not long qualified, maybe twenty-five?'

'How old were you?'

Cullen stared into the scummy coffee, at the undissolved granules. 'Twelve.'

'She was more than twice your age.'

'Right.' Cullen tried to sip the coffee but it was still too hot. 'My school did this thing where our classes went to Holland at the end of first year. And she... She was very flirtatious. Made me feel so special. All of the boys were giving it all that locker-room bollocks, you know. But she made me go to her room. Then she started kissing me. And started taking off my clothes. Made me touch her. I mean, knowing what I do now, she was very clearly in the wrong, but she made *me* feel bad. Talked about my cock being weird and all that. Made me have sex with her and tell nobody about it.' He shut his eyes. 'The next year, I was at a different school, in a different town. Just for, like, a year, then I got back and she'd left the school that summer, never heard from her again.'

'Jesus Christ, Scott. I'm glad you told me. It was

wrong what she did. And it's not your fault, okay?' Hand on his knee. 'You're not to blame. She is. Miss Carnegie. Christ.'

'It's fine.'

'No, it's very far from fine. That's really bad.'

'I mean, I've had counselling for it. After uni, just before I joined the cops. Going through it, I persuaded myself that being a cop would be how to deal with it.'

'Your parents knew?'

'Mum did. But only recently. I mean, I think I'm mostly fine. But I still have issues.'

'You ever find her?'

'No, she left.'

'But you're a cop. You could've looked her up.'

'Aye, and some things are better left in the past.'

'Right, right. But there's some closure you need to get with Miss Carnegie.'

'No, there's not.'

Yvonne wrapped an arm around him. 'It explains a lot to me.'

Cullen fell into the cuddle. 'The way I see it, the whole abuse thing is connected to trying to prove that I'm a man. All the shagger reputation stuff. That doctor, who I really like... There's something about her that triggered me. I don't know. I really like her, but something spooked me and I ran a mile. I tried texting her to break it off and thought it was all fine. Then I saw her at the hospital today and I felt so bad because she was really angry with me for not contacting her when I had the wrong number and... I had texted her. Tried calling, tried to own it all. But they'd bounced.'

'Why do you think she spooked you?'

'I think it's because she wears glasses like Miss Carnegie did.'

Christ, he was crying.

'I'm sorry to dump this on you, Yvonne.'

She held him closer. 'I'm so sorry for what happened to you, Scott. I'm glad you told me.'

'Thank you.'

20

Hunter

This close to Christmas and the cards would have you believe it would be snowing. Robins, holly, reindeer, snowmen. But not in Edinburgh. A true card would have pissing rain, drunken arseholes shouting their way home, a couple shagging in a phone box, spilled chips covered in urine, and a Santa Claus slumped against the wall by the posh light shop, completely out of his box. Sick down his front, his trousers missing but his beard and hat still intact.

Hunter should call it in, but he couldn't be arsed sorting it out himself, so he stepped past, and got out his phone.

No missed calls from Yvonne or any texts. Probably meant she was having a good time. Life and soul of the party.

He sent a text:

Working? Drunk Santa sleeping on Causewayside. Light shop

He pocketed his phone and walked past the chip shop. Looked like the owner was getting shouted at by a skinny wee bastard. Not Hunter's fight, but someone else's. He got out his phone to text in another report.

But Finlay had replied:

Hey, jabroni. Long time no hear. Aye, working. Will head up the now. City centre is a war zone. Need a break! Pint soon?

Hunter tapped the keys as he walked:

Pint would be good. And cheers. Oh, and minor stramash in chip shop

He put his phone away and got out his keys, then rounded the corner to their flat. Lights on, though, so Yvonne was back. No sounds, no music and not even her chainsaw snoring. But probably she was off her face on Sambuca and had half the team back for a nightcap and Lady Gaga on the stereo.

Just great...

Hunter unlocked the door and bent down to stroke Mrs Tuftington, rolling around on the marble floor in front of him. 'Hey, I'm glad someone's keen to see me.'

The little cat purred, then jerked upright and shot off up the staircase, ears back, tail all fluffed up.

Hunter followed the cat up, just in time to see Mrs Tuftington slip through the cat flap in old Elsie's flat door. He slid his key in the lock but didn't twist it. Just listened.

No Lady Gaga, no chat.

Strange.

He twisted the key and stepped in. Coffee smells and some light snoring, both coming from the lounge. He dropped his key in the empty dish and followed the smell.

Yvonne was sleeping on the sofa, wrapped in Scott Cullen's arms.

Just in their underwear.

Hunter dashed over and hauled Cullen off the sofa. 'What the hell are you doing?'

Yvonne thumped down on the sofa, face first. 'Craig?'

Cullen was still asleep, not even complaining as his

head bounced off the laminate. Pished out of his skull. Drooling like Ricky Falconer.

'Surprised you could get it up, you drunk wanker!' Hunter grabbed his feet and dragged him away from the sofa, along the hallway and out into the stairwell. 'You filthy bastard!' He pushed him down the stairs.

Cullen rocked and rolled his way down the steps.

Hunter stormed back in and grabbed Cullen's clothes from the floor. The shirt had a red stain. Could be wine, but probably Yvonne's lipstick.

Filthy bastard.

Filthy bastard!

He balled up the clothes and grabbed his loafers, then hurled the whole lot down the stairs, hoping the shoes hit Cullen's face and the clothes landed in a pool of Mrs Tuftington's piss.

The least he deserved.

Hunter slammed the door and stood there, fists clenched.

What the hell was he going to do?

Yvonne had been shagging Cullen in their flat. The one they'd bought together. Signed the mortgage together. Paid in equal amounts. And she shagged *him* here?

How could she?

How could *he*?

Cullen was a mate. Someone Hunter was training.

Christ. And all that shite he'd spouted about being over his womanising, well that was bollocks. Maybe Cullen and Yvonne had been going on for ages.

Shite.

No, only one thing for it.

Hunter stomped through the hall back to the living room.

Yvonne was tugging on a T-shirt, but struggled to poke her head through the hole. 'Craig?' She blinked at Hunter. 'When did you get back?'

Hunter stood there, toes curled back in his shoes. 'You shagged Scott?'

'What?'

'Scott Cullen.'

'No.'

'He was here!'

'We didn't.'

'Jesus Christ, Yvonne, I found you! In his arms!'

'Nothing happened, Craig!' She was sitting up now, but seemed way beyond drunk. Maybe already in the land of hangover.

'So why are you in your knickers?'

'The boiler's broken again. Won't shut off!'

'So you just took his clothes off, aye?'

'Craig, he walked me home. That's it.'

'It's not it! You were spooning on *our* sofa!'

'We're both pissed, Craig. He was walking me home, we got talking. That's it.'

'And you got kissing, then shagging. At least tell me you used a condom!'

'Craig! Nothing happened.'

Hunter felt it hitting him. The fringes of his vision burning away like someone set fire to a roll of film. His eyes flickering, his nostrils struggling to keep still. That tugging back into his past, into the places he didn't want to go.

He shook himself free of it. 'That's it. We're splitting up.'

'Craig, nothing happened.'

'Bullshit.' Hunter walked into the bedroom and grabbed his emergency overnight bag from the wardrobe, then stopped in the doorway, but didn't look at her. 'Going to my brother's. I'll come for my stuff later.'

21

Bain

Saturday

Hate this station. This close to Arthur's Seat and the university, it doesn't feel like the same city. Too posh for yours truly. Bunch of wankers here, too. All the cops are *useless*. Much prefer my patch down in Leith.

Only good thing going for this place is the boozer around the corner. The Cheeky Judge. Now there's a bar in which I've spent many a merry night, and many an absolutely shit-faced one.

I lean back in my chair, lifting the front legs up and

nudge McNeill to take lead, but she just sits there, playing for time like I must've taught her. Maybe.

Tell you, Ricky Falconer really doesn't look well, though. Way too thin. Like drug thin, and a stronger drug than the Valium he was caning last night. But at least he looks much healthier this morning. Bright-eyed and bushy-tailed.

See the wonders a good kip can do you for?

Not that I slept well myself. Lot going on in the old noggin, least of all this toerag hiding his even worse brother from us.

McNeill leans forward, resting on her forearms. 'Where is he, Ricky?'

Ricky looks at her, then his gaze shoots away. 'No idea who you're talking about.'

'Your brother, Ricky. Kenny.'

'No idea. Not heard from him in ages.'

'So you weren't flying to Argentina with him?'

'Not him.'

'Just going on your own, were you?'

'No. I was going with a mate. A boys' holiday. Both big fans of Boca Juniors. Much better than River Plate.' He spits into the corner of the room, but I think it's just a mock thing. I hope it is. 'Going to tour the stadium, take in a couple of games. The way it works over there is nuts, man. Apertura and Clausura, so you get two leagues in a year. Absolutely nuts. And Boca are in contention to win the Apertura. First time since the Clausura in 2008. Wanted to be there to see it happen.'

'And this mate, he wouldn't happen to be The Viper?'

But Ricky isn't looking at her. Or me. Just staring at the wall, like the plain magnolia is more interesting than an Argentinian football holiday with his mate. 'No idea who that is.'

'Alexander Drake?'

'Nope.' The slightest shrug. 'No idea.'

'Not your mate?'

'Nope.'

'See, Mr Drake flew to Argentina yesterday. He was due to stand in court for a rape trial, but the witness didn't show. Next thing, he's back out, then sods off to Argentina on a fake passport. We tried to get him in Amsterdam, but we were too late. His plane took off an hour ago. That's him gone. Ricky, were you going to meet him over there?'

'I don't know who he is.'

'He's a drug dealer, Ricky. Worked at the gym where your brother's a member.'

'Sorry. Didn't think Kenny was into working out.'

'Ricky, where is Kenny? Is he in Argentina?'

'No.'

'Was he booked on the same flight as you?'

'Can't you look?'

'We can. Thing is, Alexander Drake was flying as one David Smith. So, I doubt your brother would be flying as Kenneth Falconer, would he?'

'Guess not.'

'So, who was he flying as?'

'You're not listening. He wasn't going with us.'

'So you were going to meet Mr Drake over there?'

Ricky scratches his scrawny neck. 'Kind of.'

'What's that mean?'

'Sandy got an earlier flight. Must've paid for it.'

'You know he was in court yesterday, right?'

'So I hear.'

'He was bailed. His passport was in custody. But he fled the country.'

'Christ. I had no idea.'

'He's gone. Which is a shame as his victim won't get justice for her ordeal. But Kenny... Your brother, on the other hand, has been dealing drugs to people. There's a strain of heroin that's killing people. Fifteen and counting.'

'That's... That's awful.'

'Ricky, if there's—'

'I've no idea where he is.'

'But we found you in the flat above his shop.'

'Aye, pulling a favour for him. Keep an eye on the place while he's away.'

'And you *weren't* going to meet Kenny in Argentina?'

'Nope. See. Thing about Kenny is...' He snorts, then sniffs, then slumps back in his chair, arms folded. 'Our old man served in the Falklands. Right? Lost an arm, made him a really angry man. Used to beat the shite out of us.'

With one arm? Christ!

'Then Kenny got bigger and started to dominate. And... And Dad took his life, Mum kept on at the government to get compensation from the other side. Kenny was with her all the way. So he would never go. And Kenny blamed what happened to us on the Argies.'

'And yet you got obsessed with Argentinian football?'

Ricky looks right at us. 'Now you mention it, it is a bit weird.' Daft sod. 'Believe me, the last place Kenny'd go is Argentina.'

'And where's the first place?'

Ricky stares at McNeill for a few seconds, then scratches his neck. 'Thing is, if I tell you, he'll be really angry with me.'

'Aye, I get that. But the thing is, Ricky, I promise you I won't let him know where we got his whereabouts from.'

Ricky screws up his face tight, like he's trying to will himself out of existence, or at least out of that room. 'That stuff about the heroin is on the level?'

'Could reel off a list of victims' names.'

Ricky unscrews his face and nods at us. 'Fine.'

22

Cullen

Cullen opened his eyes and shut them again. Way too bright in here. And what the hell was that noise? Cleaning? In his flat? Was that Tom? This early on a Saturday? Christ.

He rolled over in his bed and hit his head off something. Where was the duvet?

He opened his eyes again, taking it much more carefully this time.

He wasn't at home, in his room in a flat.

No, he was in a police station.

Lying under his desk.

Shite.

And he had no idea how he'd got there. He remembered Elvis, panel-beaten at the party in that hotel. Then talking to Yvonne Flockhart. Then...

Well, at least he had clothes on. His suit. The shirt was stained red.

Wine.

But where were his shoes?

Oh. He'd been using them for a pillow.

Wanker.

He checked his watch. Half six. So bloody early. No idea how long he'd slept. Or if he'd slept instead of being in a coma.

So he'd blacked out.

That was bad.

Really, really bad.

His mouth tasted of stale wine.

And not just red, some white too. And some aniseed.

Sambuca.

Stupid, stupid bastard.

He tried to sit up, but his head felt like something had cracked in there. Felt like he'd fallen down a flight of stairs.

Christ, if he'd fallen in the station, it'd be on CCTV. Someone would be sending videos around of him making a tit of himself.

'You got lost, sunshine?'

Cullen knew the voice. That fanny DI from Leith Walk. Bain, was it? He pushed himself up to a crouch then to standing. 'Dropped a pound coin and was—'

'Aye, shite you were.' Bain laughed at him, a full-throated roar. 'You were kipping on the floor like a jakie bastard.'

'I wasn't.'

'Why haven't you got your shoes on?' He was resting against his chair back, grinning away. 'Forget it. You seen Craig Hunter?'

Cullen got a wave of nausea and saw Hunter's face, twisted with rage. Dragging him by the feet, shouting at him. He had no idea what it meant. Some kind of left-over remnant of a dream? He got onto his chair without falling off it. 'Sorry. Don't think he showed up at the party last night.'

'Buggery.' Bain scratched his moustache. He had a nasty-looking rash around it. 'Are you on duty?'

Cullen couldn't remember. He'd no idea what day it was. 'I'll see if I can find him.' Cullen spotted his mobile on the desk. He held down the 3 button and it started calling Hunter. The number didn't even ring. 'Right, he's not answering.'

'Typical.'

'Why do you need him?'

'Just, got a dunt to run and I need as many bodies as

possible. You'll do, even though you stink like a vineyard's cess pit.'

'You cleared this with Davenport?'

'No idea who he is, or if he even exists, but Big Luke says it's fine. Grab as many bodies as I need.' Bain gripped Cullen's shoulder. 'Consider yourself grabbed.'

23

Hunter

'No, Terry, no!' Hunter jerked awake and jolted upright, fists clenched, ready to lash out.

Where the hell was he?

A dark room, light bleeding through the thin curtains. Some shapes moved around, but he couldn't pick anything out, so he reached over to the side. A table. And a light on top of it. His fingers crawled up and he flicked on the switch. Both bedside lights and the overhead all blazed on. Pale purple walls, darker curtains. Walls filled with framed photographs. A tall wardrobe with the top drawer hanging open.

Aye, Hunter knew exactly where he was.

His brother's flat. The spare bedroom. And not for the first time.

The memory hit him hard, anger burning in his guts like a boiling kettle.

Yvonne cuddling in to Cullen on *their* sofa. The one he'd sworn and cursed his way through assembling one Saturday afternoon. And one Sunday morning.

How could she?

How *could* she?

Him.

Him of all people.

How could *he*?

Hunter knew Cullen's reputation, had heard it from a few sources, but put it down to exaggeration. Seeing it in person, man. They'd worked together for a year, but had been mates for a few years before that.

To betray him like that? Jesus Christ.

Would he?

Would she?

Would they?

Hunter's phone lit up on the bedside table.

Sixteen texts from Yvonne.

Forty-two missed calls.

He hated avoiding things, but he needed to keep a cool head here. Needed to focus, and maintain that focus. It was over with her.

She'd betrayed him and he needed to keep it that way.

No crawling back.

Stay the course, soldier.

But he wasn't a soldier anymore. This was civilian life. Different rules, different motivations and nothing was as it seemed.

A chap at the door. 'Craig, you okay?' Murray, sounding worried.

Hunter pulled on a T-shirt and made himself decent. 'I'm good, aye.'

The door opened but Murray didn't enter. After a pause, he stepped into the room, carrying two chunky mugs, balancing like a toddler who'd just learnt to walk. His curtains haircut framed his face. 'Made you a cup of tea, Craig.' He set one on the bedside table and perched on the other side of the bed.

Looked like dairy milk, and not the freshest, but beggars couldn't be choosers. Hunter's head was thumping like he'd been to the party and made a complete twat of himself. And tea was exactly what he needed. 'Cheers, Muz.'

'So. Who's Terry?'

'An old Army pal.'

Murray sighed. 'You still getting those flashbacks?'

'Less of them.' Hunter couldn't make any eye contact with his brother. 'Thanks for letting me stay.'

'It's what family's for, eh?' Murray walked over to the window and tore open the curtains, letting thin December light through the glass. Always had a weird light down in Leith, like it was frightened of the locals. 'You want to talk about it?'

Hunter slurped his tea. 'Not really.'

'Sure? It'll help. Don't want to bottle everything up like Mum.'

'Aye, but I don't want to be like Dad.'

Murray chuckled. 'Already way too similar.'

'Harsh.' But Hunter was grinning. Christ, that hurt worse than the tears he was suppressing. 'Bottom line is it's over between me and Yvonne.'

'Sorry to hear that. I liked her. What happened?'

'Been a long time coming. Three years and it's just been... tough.' Hunter swallowed hard. 'Really tough.'

Murray slurped his tea now. 'Had a few duff relationships myself, as you know. Ending it's always hard, but necessary.'

Hunter blew out a long breath. 'I thought she might be the one, but... I mean, we had a mortgage together. Lived together. That's way closer than I've ever let anyone get. And...' He felt the tears prickle at his nostrils. 'I'll have to find somewhere to stay for a bit.'

'You can stay here.'

'Sure?'

'Sure. Be like old times. Well, without the constant threat of Dad turning up and pissing off Mum.'

Hunter smiled a thanks. 'I don't want to cramp your style, Muz.'

'No cramping. I'm flying out to Israel on Christmas Day.'

'Really?'

'Damn straight. Beauty of non-Christian countries is it'll be like any other day. We'll be a couple of months there.'

'We?'

'All in good time, bro. We can talk while we collect your stuff from the flat.'

Hunter nodded. 'I hope Yvonne can buy me out. Don't want to go through the hassle of selling it.'

'Well, you've got time. Have this place all to yourself till March.'

'Cheers. I really appreciate it.' Hunter felt that peaceful yawn, the one that made everything tingle. All the tension in his body released. 'I'll buy you a—'

Hunter's phone blasted out *Don't Look Back In Anger* by Oasis. Luke Shepherd.

Oh Christ, what did he want?

'Better take this.' Hunter put his tea down on the coaster and picked up the phone, answering it as Murray left him with a tilt of his mug. 'Sarge?'

'Craig, sorry to do this but I need you to come in to work today.'

Hunter wished he was back in that dream, back in the heat of Iraq, feeling his skin burn. The army didn't give you much freedom if any, so it couldn't be so easily taken away. Unlike the police. 'Sarge, it's a Saturday and there was the Christmas party last night.'

'Aye, and we've got two big cases on. And you weren't even at the party, so don't play that card, son. It's beneath you. I need you to pitch up today.'

Hunter drained his mug and got a mouthful of tea leaves. Christ. He spat it back out. 'I'll need to get away around lunchtime.'

Shepherd sighed down the line. 'Fine. But I need you to make sure Elvis is fit enough to work. And drive. Prick was off his face last night.'

'Aye, aye. So what's the emergency?'

'Getting a ton of heat on finding Becky Crawford. Given Alex Drake's in the wind, certain parties are concerned she's been killed.'

24

Cullen

The road seemed to veer in a million different directions. Cullen tried to blink away the fatigue, but it was inside his head now. At least he'd drunk some coffee, some water and had some painkillers. All within the maximum dose.

'Have a slug of this bad boy.' Bain handed him a can of WakeyWakey. 'Cures anything, trust me.'

'Thanks.' Cullen cracked the ring pull without checking the ingredients first. It smelled like bubblegum, but it was ice cold and hyper-caffeinated. He sucked down a drink and it tasted like second-hand bubblegum. A real struggle to keep it down, but he forced another glug as they cleared the bridge over the

Water of Leith, powering along Queensferry Road at a rapid clip. 'Where we going?'

'Drylaw.'

'And this just gets worse.' Cullen took another sip and felt the caffeine starting to surge in his veins. And his heart thud in his chest. 'Who we going for?'

'Kenny Falconer.'

Cullen frowned. 'Thought you were getting him last night?'

'Dunt was a bust. Got his brother, mind.' Bain reached into his door pocket for his own can of Wakey-Wakey, rhubarb and custard flavoured. 'Wee toerag was off his coupon on Valium, but once he sobered up, he started speaking.' He popped the ring pull with a hiss that Cullen couldn't determine the source of, can or man, then slurped it all down in a oner, then crushed the can. 'God's own drink that, I swear.' He burped.

'It's certainly helping.'

'Guessing you blacked out last night?'

Cullen shot a glare over at him, his veins burning with acid. 'What?'

'Well, I was watching you a while. And you've no idea where you were when you came to. And when you sleep under your desk, it's because nocturnal you decided the station floor was better than trying to get a cab home. Ergo, you blacked out last night.'

Cullen looked out of the window, trying to avoid staring anywhere near him. 'I'm fine.'

'No, you're not fine. Not even sure you should be here with me, but we are where we are.'

Cullen held out his hand, flat in mid-air and steady like a ten-year-old. 'I'm sober as a judge.'

'Aye, but hungover as a criminal defence lawyer.' Bain shook his head, wafting rhubarb crumble over Cullen. 'People drink to forget. What are you trying to forget, sunshine?'

'Just dealing with some issues, that's all. And it's complicated. '

'Hear that a lot.' Bain burped into his fist. 'Personal or professional?'

'Both.'

'You can talk to me, son. Especially if it's professional.'

Cullen didn't know if he could trust him. Then again, a DI asking you about your career had to be something in his favour. He let out a sigh. 'I'm a Training DC, but it feels like my career's dead in the water.'

'And why do you think that?'

'Tenure's up soon. So I'll be bumped back to uniform.'

'Care to explain to me why that's a bad thing?'

Cullen finished his drink and crushed the can, just

like Bain had. 'I joined the police because I want to change things, to be active. When I was out in West Lothian, I was this close,' he squeezed his thumb and finger together, 'to promotion. Uniform Sergeant, based in Bathgate.'

'But?'

'But my sickness record stood against me.'

'How bad was it?'

'For a couple of years it felt like my body was working against me. I was genuinely ill. Infections and weird stuff like that. Shift work didn't agree with me. But I'm on lots of vitamins and supplements at Craig's recommendation. Not had a day off in two years.'

'That's good. Six months as Training, aye?'

'Up next month.'

'Still, that kind of record won't get you into being a detective either.'

'Nope. And I'll be back in uniform.'

'How about the people side of things?'

Cullen shrank in his seat. 'Well, I think I pissed off a few people.'

'How?'

'Well, showing them up. Doing the job.'

Bain laughed. 'Aye, bollocks.'

'Seriously. Check my record.'

'That the drink talking?'

'No. I'm a really good cop.'

'Let me guess, you were on a squad with a load of fifteen-plus guys, right? And even though you're always doing good work, they treat you like their lacky. "Get us a cup of tea, Cullen. Milk, no sugar. Wife says I'm sweet enough." Oh, and "No, no, you walk the beat, sunshine, you're too new to have a motor." Oh, and "Sunshine will do all the shite jobs.".'

'Pretty much that, but please don't call me sunshine.'

Bain chuckled. 'So how did you end up in CID?'

I put in for a transfer from Bathgate to Edinburgh and...' He sighed. 'Got knocked back. Then I worked a case, and caught Davenport's attention, and Craig put in the recommendation.'

'So, why are you here, in this situation?'

'What situation?'

'Heading back to uniform?'

'I don't know.'

'But it hurts, right?'

'Agony.'

'Right in the guts, eh?' Bain reached over and play-punched Cullen's shoulder. 'Ambition is good, son. Nothing wrong with it. Got me where I am. Any senior officer too. And it puts you in control of your trauma.'

'My *trauma*?'

'We've all got trauma, son. All carrying some shite. Just make sure you're in control of it.' Bain turned into a side street, two rows of ex-council houses separated by a big green in the middle. Big enough for a football pitch, but just bare grass now. Satellite dishes on both sides, fancy cars shining in the morning gloom, still an hour before sunrise, still half an hour before they headed to work. Bain pulled up and got out first. 'Look lively.'

Cullen followed him out into the freezing cold. It hit him like a snow shovel in the face. Maybe it was that or the WakeyWakey, but he was feeling a bit more human, even if he still had no idea what the hell he'd been up to last night. He scanned the street. 'Which one is it?'

'Don't you think they might notice a bunch of cops showing up outside?' Bain shook his head. 'Round the corner, you daft sod.' He was pointing to a familiar face. 'ADC Cullen, meet DS Sharon McNeill.'

Cullen nodded at her. 'You arrested me at the gym.'

'Aye, that's right.' Bain's eyes were glinting with mischief. 'She absolutely battered you, as I recall. How about I call you Butch, and Cullen here can be your Sundance Kid?'

McNeill scowled at him. 'Do what you want.'

'Always do.' Bain put his radio to his lips. 'Al, you in position? Over.'

It crackled, sounded like a 'Not yet.'

'Christ's sake.' Bain pressed the button again. 'Then get your arse in gear. Over.'

25

Hunter

Hunter eased up the old railway line that continued the Western Approach Road into deepest, darkest Gorgie. At least, he thought it was an old railway line. Could just be a weird road.

'All over my suit.' Elvis was rubbing his chest. 'I mean, who throws up over someone else?'

Hunter gripped the wheel tight as he powered west. 'Sure it wasn't you chucking up on yourself?'

'Craig, I'd know if I'd been sick all over myself.' Elvis frowned. Christ, he looked like he'd just got back from a very restful holiday. 'Funny thing was, the taxi driver didn't ask for any money.'

'What, for being sick?'

'I wasn't sick.' Elvis shook his head and sighed. 'No, for the fare. That's weird, eh?'

'Sounds like someone shoved you into a taxi, Paul.'

'That can't be right. Who'd do that for me?' Elvis was positively beaming. 'I feel fresh as a daisy today.' He yawned into his fist, then scanned the street they hurtled down. 'You missed a good night, though. Cracking fun.'

'Bet you did too.' Hunter pulled up at the lights. Not many cars up ahead, so he could just sneak it when they changed. He caught Elvis's yawn, though, one of those that made you shut your eyes and didn't let go for ages. He'd barely slept. Murray really needed to fix that lumpy bed and the thin curtains. But how did you explain that to someone giving you a roof over your head? Maybe he should buy one and repay the favour that way? 'Did you check the address?'

'Yvonne did. Last night.'

'Remind me.'

'Rebecca Crawford. Becky to her pals. Me and Yvonne managed to find her landlord last night. Wee boy down in Leith, owns a few places in Porty. But said landlord grumbled like a bastard, until she threatened him. Anyhoo, he found Becky's form and dropped it off at the station this morning. Yvonne's not in but, lo and behold, there's an address for her parents, out here in Ravelston.'

The light shifted yellow and Hunter hit the pedal, then shot round the bend. 'Fancy.'

'Could say that, aye.' Elvis did another yawn. 'How was she this morning?'

Hunter ignored him and just drove, past two competing chip shops and a pub he'd broken up a fight in many years ago. Two red-faced old buggers tearing lumps out of each other over a betting slip. Supposed to be where the grave diggers drank in times gone by.

'Yvonne was getting very cosy with Cullen.'

'Was she?'

'Aye.'

'Shut up, Elvis.'

'Seriously, I hate that name.' Elvis ran a finger down his sideburns, like he was measuring them for size. 'And I'm just winding you up. She turned up just as I left. I think. But cosy is the word I'd use.'

'Good for her.'

'Don't you live with her, Craig?'

'I did, aye.'

'What?'

Hunter sped along the road and weaved around a cyclist going barely above walking speed. 'I don't want to talk about it.'

'Come on, mate. I'm just messing with you.'

'Well, it's time to stop messing and just shut up.'

'Ooooo-ooh!'

'Seriously.'

'Look, Craig, I'm just worried. Got a text from your brother. Murray said you were staying at his last night. Everything okay?'

'Just needed a change of scene, that's all.'

'Suuure.' Aye, Elvis believed it as much as Hunter.

'I got held back with Bain, supporting his foiled raid on a bookshop. Didn't want Yvonne coming in hammered after the do and waking me up.'

'Aye, so you left the door open for young Cullen.'

Hunter could throttle the daft sod. Could do worse to his brother for grassing to Elvis of all people. Silence was the best policy here.

'You two were good for each other, that's all.'

'I agree on the past tense. And we weren't. This has been on the cards for a long while.'

'What, her letting young Cullen into her knickers?'

'Paul, shut up.'

Elvis raised his hands. 'Know when to quit, don't I?'

No. He really didn't. Never did.

Part of what made him a decent cop, but also what made him an annoying wanker.

'Next left.'

Hunter had to slam on the brakes to stop in time.

Got a blast of horn from behind. 'Could've done with some warning.'

'Thought you knew.'

'You said Ravelston. This is Coates Avenue.'

'Same difference.'

'It's miles apart.' Hunter huffed out a sigh. No point in arguing. He was driving much more slowly now, the needle barely hitting fifteen. Tall beech hedges on both sides, their winter leaves all brown, interspersed with the occasional railings. Big mature trees hid the houses from view. One of those Edinburgh streets with no real identity, just massive old houses set in massive grounds. And too early for the parking spaces to be occupied or the drives to be emptied. 'Which number?'

Elvis pointed. 'That one.'

Great. The one house covered in scaffolding. Two vans either side of the drive. Still, there were signs of life. Someone who might know where Becky Crawford was.

Hunter couldn't believe it had taken them this long to get an address, but judging by these houses, maybe that wasn't a surprise. Pay through the nose for the privacy. Probably educated privately, so there's no local footprint. Shop in town or at a big supermarket on the outskirts. Barely living here.

Hunter got out and hit the din, the rattle and thump of scaffolding poles being transported and slotted into place. The tinny rasp of chart dance music as knuckle-dragging Neanderthals boogied to the campest love songs, singing along together.

'Be careful!' A chunky man in a suit stood by the front door, clutching an espresso cup between thumb and forefinger, his pinky jutting out. 'We just had the windows replaced last year.'

'Aye, aye.' The biggest, ugliest scaffolder. One who'd give Hunter a run for his money in terms of size and looks. 'Do this aw day, every day, pal. We're careful as—'

CLANG.

'Sorry!' A topless wee skinny bugger was clutching his foot, the pole he'd dropped rolling away from him. 'Ah, you—'

'Stevie!' The big boss man clipped his ear. 'Get it picked up and up that ladder before I ram my toe right up your crevice again.' He smiled at Mr Espresso. 'Sorry, sir. We are careful.'

'Hmm.'

Hunter spotted his opportunity and got between them, warrant card out. 'Mr Crawford?'

'Aye.' He looked him up and down. 'How can I help?'

'Police, sir.' Hunter kept his warrant card there, given how detailed an inspection it was getting. 'DC Craig Hunter. DC Paul Gordon.' Though there was no sign of Elvis. Great. 'Looking for a Rebecca Crawford.'

'I see.' Crawford threw his espresso down his neck, then wiped his lips. 'Well, she's not here.'

'When did you—'

'Moved out when she was sixteen, didn't she?' Crawford gritted his teeth and narrowed his eyes. 'After all we've done for her. Six years ago, she just grabbed a bag and buggered off.' Just like Hunter last night. 'Little madam, I tell you.'

'Do you—'

'No, I have no idea where she could be.'

Hunter looked inside the house. The hallway seemed like a show home, bare floorboards and pristine bookcases filled with all the best coffee table books. The living room was empty, just a pair of sofas facing each other. No telly, but two giant paintings on adjacent walls. He looked back at Crawford. 'Mind if we have a look inside?'

'Are you calling me a liar?'

'Sir, if she's here, we—'

'Believe me, I wouldn't let her in if she begged.'

'Those are just words, sir.'

'I'm not letting you in here either without a warrant.'

Bloody hell.

Elvis had appeared, yawning into his fist and blinking away some tiredness.

Hunter smiled. 'Cool.' He patted Elvis on the arm.

'Let's get Ally on the phone. Be, what, lunchtime before we get the warrant signed? Then we can get the biggest, ugliest buggers on the force to tear this place apart. Be *hours* searching a house like this. And we'll sit opposite, watching for his daughter running off, aye?'

'Don't you think you can intimidate me.'

'Just need to find your daughter, sir. She's gone missing.'

'Well, I honestly don't care.'

'That's cold.'

'*She* did this to *us*. As far as we're concerned, we no longer have a daughter.'

'Any sons?'

'None. Now, kindly bugger off and get a warrant. I've got to get to the gallery for opening.'

Hunter smiled as he handed over a business card. 'We'll just be in the car over the road, watching your house until we get that warrant.'

Folded arms, deep scowl. 'By all means.'

'Be seeing you.' Hunter walked back to the car and got in. Then bit his thumbnail until Elvis got in. 'We're screwed.'

'Aye. Thought you had him there, but nope. You believe him?'

'Seems a bit cold, but then a place like that, a house like this? Can believe anything.' Hunter got out his phone and called Shepherd.

Two rings and he had an ear full of mouth breathing. 'Craig, where are you?'

'Following up on Becky Crawford's whereabouts, Sarge. Need a warrant to access a property in Coates Avenue.'

'Aye, aye. I'll speak to Ally, but you're in a good position. I need you at a raid at a house in Drylaw. That cowboy idiot Bain has gone off the reservation on something. Taken half my team without asking me!'

26

Cullen

Sundance Kid?

Christ.

Cullen hoped that didn't stick. He walked down the street, following in Bain's slipstream. The rain was hammering down so heavily now it sluiced down the side of the street, avoiding the drains and spreading out towards the middle of the road. And he was soaked through already. On the plus side, the icy chill seemed to help the hangover.

Two uniform cars blocked the end of the road, barring any traffic except those with the post-apocalyptic look of old pool cars. And the craned necks of nosy plainclothes officers.

Talk about subtle.

The lead uniform was talking to an old woman dragging a suitcase behind her, presumably a makeshift shopping trolley. Arms folded across his chest, black T-shirt turned up at the cuffs to show off his biceps, though puckered with gooseflesh, and tight enough to show the contours of his beer gut. And with that harsh glistening black you only got from standing in the rain. 'Just doing some door-to-door work, ma'am.'

Cullen recognised him. PC Finlay Sinclair. Bit of a twat, best to be avoided. Actually, a total arsehole. One of the worst for getting "young Cullen" to make his tea. Dick.

Cullen caught up with Bain and McNeill, huddling under a Standard Life brolly. 'So, what's the plan here?'

A pool car pulled up alongside. Hunter got out, scowling like he'd got out of bed the wrong side that morning. 'Bastard thing needs to be taken apart and used for scrap.'

Cullen grinned at him. 'Poor workman blames his tools, Craig.'

Hunter didn't even look at Cullen, instead staring straight at Bain. 'Luke's wondering why you're bouncing his calls.'

Bain reached into his pocket with a deep frown, then got out his phone. 'Well, would you believe it? A ton of missed calls from an unknown number. Usually don't answer them. Could be one of those PPI scammers, you know?'

'He's on his way over. Wants you to wait.'

'And I want to win the lottery. Neither are going to happen.'

'Said you've stolen half of his team for an unapproved mission.'

Bain rubbed his moustache. 'Thing is, Craig my man, Luke might be a DS, but I'm a DI so I don't take orders from him.' He put his radio to his thin lips. 'Al, tell me you're in place.'

'Aye, Ferry Road's locked down.'

Bain stared round at Finlay, with the old wifie wandering away from him, her suitcase trundling behind him. 'You got the Big Key, aye?'

'Sir.' Finlay held up a battering ram, his arm muscles straining with the effort. A peal of water sprayed off it.

Bain focused on Cullen, then Hunter. 'Lads, you can wait for your daddy to pitch up, or you can see how a pro does it. Choice is yours.'

Cullen tried to make eye contact with Hunter, but he was getting nowhere. What was his problem? He still had a vision of that dream where Hunter hauled him around. Had to be an anxiety dream.

And Bain was right. Blacking out wasn't good, especially when it meant he was dreaming up weird shit like that.

Hunter's lips twisted into a scowl. 'Fine.'

'Fine, you're coming with, or fine you're grassing on me?'

'Coming with. Let's get this out of the way. And it's your obbo, not ours. So when this goes south, it's on you.'

Cullen stepped forward, close to Hunter. 'I'm in too.'

'Sweet.' Bain held up his radio again. 'We are go!' He set off past the cars.

Cullen kept pace with Elvis, splashing in the fresh puddles. 'Was Craig blanking me there?'

'Did he break your heart?' Elvis was grinning. 'Or maybe he found you banging his girlfriend?'

'Shut up. Nothing happened.'

'Oh aye? There's something going on?'

'I walked her home. She was hammered, that was it.'

Up ahead, Bain stopped outside a block of flats and held up a hand. 'Steady.'

Finlay leaned in and whisper-shouted, 'It's not here.'

'What?'

'The address.' Finlay waved behind the flats. 'Old shop over there.'

'Bloody hell.' Bain shook his head and darted down a side lane.

Cullen followed, just behind Hunter and McNeill, then emerged into a car park. In the middle, an old three-storey brick building huddled in the downpour, boarded-up windows battered by the rain. Just those three little words above to indicate what it would've been when open. Beers. Wines. Spirits. Would've been a goldmine at some point, but the massive Tesco and Morrisons nearby clearly undercut the business. No sign of any CCTV, so if Kenny Falconer was in there, he was there covertly.

Finlay dropped his ram by a metal roll-down gate. 'Fat lot of use this is going to be.'

Cullen rounded the corner and was a bit stunned to be on Ferry Road. He felt like he'd jumped a few streets, but there it was. A steady flow of traffic, even at this time of day. Headlights and brake lights glowing through the drizzle. A few squad cars sat there, marking the territory, but maybe that was par for the course for half eight on a Friday morning. Prime fighting time. The mobility scooters were all parked outside the bookies, no doubt ready for the pilgrimage along to the gritty boozer. The shops further along were open. The building had a long balcony running along outside the upstairs offices. All lights off up there, most of the windows boarded up.

Weird, weird place.

'Bloody hell.' Bain was ruffling his moustache, then pointed at the bookies. 'Get in there and see if we can barge through!'

Cullen set off round to the back entrance.

No sign of Finlay or his battering ram, except for a shout: 'Sir!'

Cullen shot off in that direction.

Finlay was standing by a back door, cradling the ram like a newborn. 'This is it.'

Cullen tried the damp door handle, but it was locked. Wouldn't even rattle. He looked back the way and caught a glower from Bain. 'Sir, shall we—'

'Bloody get in there!'

'Wanker.' Finlay pressed the battering ram against the door. 'Heave ho!' He engaged it and it sank its teeth into the wood, sending the door toppling inside. Finlay planted himself against the side wall to let the others past.

Cullen was first in, baton raised, charging into a long corridor. Dark, damp and smelling of mould.

Ahead was a staircase leading up.

McNeill blocked the entrance. 'Secure the other two doors.'

Hunter took the right, shining his torch around a storeroom. Looked empty, just a few empty cans of lager.

Cullen took the other one, into the shop. The counter was still there, a plastic-y thing that ran the length of the shop. Some old fridges against both outside walls, empty and dead. Next door's bookie's TV droned through the walls. No sign of anyone or anything behind the till. 'Clear!' He went back into the hallway.

McNeill pointed at Elvis, then at the shop door. 'Guard that.' She nodded at Cullen. 'You, follow me.'

Cullen walked up the stairs after McNeill and stepped out into an office space. One door, loads of windows, mostly boarded up. A few desks and office chairs.

McNeill touched a finger to her lips and took the left side, leaving Cullen to take the other. 'Up here!'

Cullen darted over to her position.

A woman sat on a sagging couch, eyes wide with shock and maybe relief. Long hair, tied loosely in a ponytail. Trousers, blouse, both black.

McNeill stood next to her, keeping her secure, and reached out a hand. 'You okay, Becky?'

Becky Crawford.

That didn't make any sense. She'd been due to testify against Falconer's associate, so why would she be here? Was he holding her?

McNeill leaned in close to her. 'Are you okay?'

'I thought he was going to kill me.' Becky looked

like she hadn't slept all year. Deep lines under her eyes like used teabags. 'He was making sure I didn't testify against... *him*. They kidnapped me. He was going to kill me.'

'Who?'

'Kenny.'

'Becky, is he here?'

She frowned, then her eyes shot over to the door.

'Get after him!' McNeill stared at Cullen and pointed to the right.

Christ.

Eyes on the prize, hangover boy.

Cullen gripped his baton and inched towards the door. Then stopped to listen. Just water dripping somewhere. The light was faint, but his eyes had adjusted to it now. And just smashing; a three-way split here. A toilet up ahead, and more offices to the right.

Left was a big open-plan space, with the few windows still containing glass shining bright.

Kenny Falconer stood in the middle of the room, brandishing a knife. 'You can leave while you still have your balls.'

Cullen stepped into the room. 'Kenneth Falconer, I'm arresting you under suspicion of supplying a controlled substance.'

'Aye, bollocks to that.' Falconer jolted forward,

lashing out with his knife and slicing the air in front of Cullen.

Shite!

Cullen swiped with his baton, but only caught tracksuit bottoms.

Pain flared up from his balls, internal fire singeing up his guts and down his legs. Felt like he was going to throw up. And he went down to his knees. A crack off his cheekbone.

And footsteps raced out of the room.

Christ.

He'd made a right arse of this.

27

Hunter

Whatever magic beans Ricky Falconer had sold them, it hadn't led to a beanstalk, just to an empty store room. The whole shop was empty. And had been for a good while.

Well, almost empty — Elvis had found a box of Snickers bars and was tucking into one. '*Ravenous.*'

Ricky Falconer... Another lie from a subhuman scumbag. Or, if Hunter was being generous, his intel was twelve hours out of date.

Maybe if Hunter had been allowed to—

Get over yourself, Craig.

'Up here!' A woman's voice. That hard-arse DS who worked for that fanny Bain. 'Both of you!'

Hunter clambered up the stairs, baton raised, into an office. Hard to figure out who'd need an office here, but that was a mystery for another time.

McNeill was crouching by a tattered old couch, next to a woman who looked a lot like Becky Crawford.

'What the hell are—'

'Go!' McNeill was pointing behind him. 'Your sidekick has gone after Falconer.'

Just fantastic.

Cullen. Against Falconer. Talk about being outmatched.

'On it.' Hunter powered on, grabbing his baton so tight it'd leave an imprint in his palm. And he'd need it. He knew Falconer, knew he was a knife guy. A quick smack to the forearm would loosen his wrist, shake the blade free. And an unarmed Falconer was just a skinny little sod with anger issues.

Hunter stopped outside the doorway and waited for Elvis to join him. Quiet through there. Thin light, revealing a three-way junction. No clues as to which way they'd gone. Wait, what was that? Sounded like someone was groaning.

He snapped out his baton, then gave Elvis a nod of three, then stepped around the corner into another office space. Three windows up ahead, all overlooking Ferry Road.

Heavy breathing and loud moans.

Cullen lay on the floor, clutching his balls.

Hunter raced over to him. 'Where did he go?'

'No idea.' Cullen inched up to kneeling, but he was acting like his stomach had been kicked through his spinal column. Always one for exaggeration.

'Useless twat.' Hunter took another look around. Only one door out of there. Footsteps rattled a floorboard through there.

Cullen tried to join him, but just couldn't.

Hunter put a finger to his lips.

Glass smashed.

Hunter walked over to the door, baton raised. A wash of cold, a taste of rain on the air. He tore open the door, ready to lash out.

The room was empty. No sign of Falconer. Curtains flapped by the window.

Hunter stepped over to the window, still holding his baton. The glass was smashed and biting air lapped at his face.

And there he was.

Kenny Falconer was out on the ledge above the shops, staring down at the squad cars, like he was checking for any gaps in the defensive wall.

Hunter could see it — bounce down onto a car roof, then down the bonnet and onto the street, then shoot across the road. Lose himself in the housing schemes either side of the main road. As well as a knife guy,

Falconer was a runner. He'd outstrip any of the cops in seconds, maybe with the exception of Cullen.

No.

Falconer was going down.

Hunter stuck a leg through the smashed window, and a searing burst of pain climbed his arm. His shirt was torn open and a gash ran down the outside of his forearm. Idiot. He bit his teeth down and tried to keep his whimpering to himself, then put his other leg out onto the ledge. The teeming rain streamed off his face. Thick, heavy and ice cold.

Falconer was still staring down, but was rocking back and forward, like he was timing his jump.

'Stop!' Hunter lurched towards Falconer, baton raised and ready to swipe.

But Falconer clocked him, and swung around, swiping out with his knife.

Hunter ducked under the blow, and smashed Falconer in the kidney with his free hand.

A sharp elbow caught Hunter in the face and he went down. His baton clattered onto the balcony, then started rolling towards the edge.

Hunter reached out for the baton, but it tumbled down onto street below.

Falconer was on him, though, playing with the knife, swiping it through the air. All for show, trying to instil maximum fear.

Hunter hopped up to standing and got a blast of pain down his arm. 'Kenny Falconer, I'm arresting you for supp—'

Falconer slashed out with the knife.

Hunter just managed to skip out of the way in time. He stepped back, trying to keep his distance. A knife versus a baton was one thing, but a knife against fists? Forget it. 'Why was Becky here? Were you going to kill her?'

Falconer's eyes were shooting all over Hunter, his knife hand tracking the motion. 'Who cares about her?'

'Her parents?'

'Don't kid yourself, arsehole. Her folks hate her.'

'You should hand yourself over now, Kenny. Let me arrest you. Then you can do time for supplying deadly drugs to people.'

'Not me.'

'From Rock Hard Gym. We know it was you.'

'Piss off.' Falconer jerked the knife towards his throat.

Hunter was quicker this time, dodging the swipe and grabbing hold of Falconer's wrist. A sharp tug and Falconer slipped forward, tipping facedown onto the balcony. The knife rattled against the wall.

Hunter still had hold of the wrist. He twisted it around, trying to pull it up Falconer's back. He stepped around and something under his feet rocked. Hunter tried to right himself, but he slipped on the slick surface and his back cracked off the window pane. He fell on his side, landing on his sore arm. Screaming out in pain.

'You stupid bastard!' Falconer kneeled on him, knees locking both arms down and pressing him against the wet balcony. He lowered the knife to Hunter's throat.

28

Cullen

Cullen's balls were on fire.

Christ, it felt like something had snapped down there.

He sucked in a breath deep enough to let him stand up.

Focus.

Where did Hunter go?

That door. He hadn't come back out. So, he must be in there. Right?

He managed to waddle over to the doorway and looked through. No sign of anyone in there, so he stepped in.

The window. It was smashed, letting in the cold morning rain.

Cullen wheezed over to the breeze and peeked out. A pile of smashed glass lay on the balcony. The noses of three squad cars down below.

Kenny Falconer lay on top of Hunter, knees pinning his arms down.

Hunter was struggling and trying to buck him off with strong hip thrusts, but Falconer was winning.

Metal glinted in the harsh light.

Knife!

Cullen used his baton to free the rest of the broken glass, then eased through the window. The rain lashed his forehead, his cheeks, his mouth. His clothes were soaked. He stepped towards the wrestling pair, his baton clenched in both hands. Taking care to focus and time his strike perfectly.

Now.

He lashed out and connected steel with Falconer's forearm. The knife spilled and Cullen kicked out, cracking his soggy shoe into Falconer's head. Pushing him against the wall.

Dazed. Stunned. Hungry fingers reached for his knife.

Hunter jolted upright, then got on top of Falconer, fist raised above his face. 'People are dying because of you!' He smashed a fist into his face. 'Do you remember Angus?'

Falconer spat blood at Hunter.

Another punch. 'Angus Henderson.'

Cullen grabbed Hunter's arm. 'Craig! Stop it!'

Falconer was grinning wide. 'Remind me?'

'You bullied him.' Hunter shook free of Cullen's grip. 'He killed himself.'

Falconer laughed. 'Not my fault he let his uncle bugger him.'

'It's your fault he jumped in front of a train!' Hunter shifted to strangling Falconer. 'All the abuse, the teasing. All from you and your mates. Then you chased after him, shouting about how he was a paedo. Then he killed himself. You're going to pay for it!'

'Craig!' Cullen grabbed Hunter's shoulders, pulling him back. 'You'll kill him!'

'That's kind of the point.' Hunter pushed Cullen away with his free hand, a thick smack against his chest. 'This prick is killing people and he just doesn't care! He killed my friend!' Tears streamed down his cheeks. 'He did it. Made him do it! Bullied him! Made his life hell! Made him jump in front of a train!'

Falconer was a bloody pulp. Cuts above both eyes, blood running down his cheeks. His mouth was like something from the butcher. 'Can't make anyone do anything.' His eyes were awake, alert. He reached to the side and—

'Knife!' Cullen pulled Hunter towards the wall and the knife cut through the air.

Missed.

Falconer was on his feet now, still holding the knife. He lashed out at Hunter, making Hunter skip out of the way.

And straight into Cullen, pushing him back. Cullen bounced off a boarded-up window and stumbled forward towards the ledge, and stepped right over.

The dark sky spun around and Cullen hit something hard, with a dark thud. A car alarm blasted out.

Cullen couldn't move. Every bit of his body felt like it'd been through a mincer.

'You little shite!' Above him, Hunter had Falconer in his arms, turned upside down. Looked like he was going to throw him.

'Craig! No!' But Cullen's cry was a feeble squeak.

And Hunter didn't pay any attention.

Falconer sailed through the air, heading right for Cullen.

Cullen tried to move as much as he could, but he was a broken mess. Falconer landed on his hip. Cullen screamed, but tried to grab hold of him. Falconer bounced off onto the tarmac.

He was going to get away!

Cullen tried to get up, tried to follow, but he just couldn't move.

Hunter was standing above, up on the balcony. Staring at Cullen, but not seeing him. All he had to do was hop down and he could get Falconer.

But he was gone, lost to some memory.

Shepherd raced out of the bookies, baton drawn, then stopped dead, his mouth hanging open. 'Christ!'

Cullen rolled forward on the car so he was at least sitting. 'Arrest him!'

29

Hunter

Hunter stared along the row of shops, all technically open but hidden behind a police cordon. The rain had abated a bit and just left an ice-cold wind. Another two ambulances sat there. A flash of lights, a blast of siren and one shot off along Ferry Road. Maybe he should look down again.

Just in time to see the paramedic dig a needle into Hunter's arm and pull the thread through. 'Usually use staples in a case like this, but your skin's a bit funny.'

Hunter tried to bite through the sharp, stinging pain. 'Funny?'

'Aye, not quite sticking together. Like leather. Has your skin been tanned?'

'Not since Iraq.'

The paramedic laughed, then snapped off the thread and tied it off. 'Anyway, that's you.'

'That's it?'

'Aye, you'll need to go to your GP in five days.' He patted Hunter's arm. 'And watch what you're doing around broken glass. Has a tendency to slice open your arms.' He stared deep into Hunter's eyes. 'And you should get a blood test.'

'A test?'

'HIV, hepatitis, the full spectrum.' He thumbed over at the other ambulance. 'From what I gather, the lad you were wrestling with up there, he's a dealer. Heroin. If I was you, I'd assume he uses his product and I'd assume he isn't very discriminatory about who he shares needles with. Get the test, know the truth. And deal with it.'

'Not my first rodeo.' Hunter couldn't look into his eyes so stared up at the ambulance's roof instead. 'Not the first time someone's blood mixed with mine.' But that was it. He couldn't share any more.

'Must be tough, but get the test and you'll be fine. That girlfriend of yours will be okay with it.'

'What girlfriend?'

'Wee Yvonne.'

Hunter clamped his eyes shut. 'She's not my girlfriend.'

He frowned. 'Saw her just yesterday and she—'

'We split up last night.'

'Oh, sorry to hear that.' He stepped back. 'Right, well. You're good to go, Craig. Be careful out there.'

'Will do. Cheers.' Hunter grabbed his coat and stepped out into the morning air, just as the rain hit again, coming down like prison bars. It caressed him like a lover, that dirty cold against his cheeks, running its hands through his hair.

He looked over at the row of shops. Forensics were up on the roof, working away inside too. God knows what they were going to find.

But at least it wasn't Falconer's dead body. No, his live one was heading to the infirmary.

And Hunter had almost killed him.

Something had snapped in him. He'd tried to murder him. Thrown him off the roof, head first.

And there was a huge part of him that wished he'd succeeded.

Not least as repayment for what that little worm did to Angus. Happened when Hunter was abroad, fighting the good fight. Falconer and his mates, bullying the local weirdo. Not knowing the traumas Angus had endured, the abuse. And Hunter wasn't around to protect him.

Still, Falconer was going to prison for a good stretch. Once they started digging, they might pin those two murders on him, the ones Chantal couldn't.

Either way, Kenny Falconer wasn't going to be anybody's problem for a very long time.

'Craig.'

Hunter swung around.

Shepherd was huddling under an Alba Bank golf brolly. 'You okay?'

Hunter held out his arm, but his bandage was hidden by his jacket. 'Got off pretty lightly.'

'Saw the other guy. Saw what you did to him.' Shepherd stomped over to Hunter, his lips smacking as he chewed gum. Hunter could taste his peppermint in the damp air. 'Stupid, stupid bastard.' He waved a hand at the spot the other ambulance had been in. 'What were you thinking, battering him like that?'

'Trust me, I got the worst of it.'

'Aye? Because you look like you've just got out of the sauna or steam room, whereas he looks like a mine's exploded on him. A six foot four mine.'

Hunter took a deep breath. 'Sarge, he pulled a knife on me. Knocked my baton to the ground below... knife versus fists is not usually a winning combination, eh?'

Shepherd barked out a laugh. 'Sorry, I forgot that gives you an excuse for trying to kill him.'

'I didn't try to—'

'Tossing someone off a balcony isn't trying to kill someone?'

Hunter held his glare. 'He slipped.'

'DC Gordon saw it, you daft sod. You threw him.' Shepherd shook his head. 'Craig, Ally wants to do you for going over the score here. Okay, so we caught Falconer, but you almost killed him when you arrested him. Any lawyer worth his salt will get this thrown out of court.'

'It wasn't that way at all.' Cullen, limping like he was missing one or both testicles. Or had grown a third one. He pointed up at the roof and winced with the effort. 'I was up there with them, trying to help arrest the suspect. The truth was, Falconer would've killed either of us. Maybe both. He was going to slit Craig's throat. Then Falconer threw me down onto the car.'

Shepherd looked over at the squad car, the roof crumpled from the impact of two idiots hitting it. 'So why does DC Gordon think that's not what happened?'

Cullen shrugged. 'Search me, Sarge. But Craig wouldn't do that.'

Hunter folded his arms, but the searing burn up his arm stopped him. 'The way I saw it, Falconer was going for his knife, which he'd spilled. Then he slipped, I tried to grab him and he fell.'

Shepherd stared hard at Cullen for a few seconds. 'If you're lying to me, Scott, I swear to God... So help me, but being back in uniform will be the least of your worries.'

'Clear off, Luke.' DI Bain was leaning against the side of the ambulance, hand resting on a hip. 'They're telling the truth.'

'You saw it?'

Bain nodded. 'I was up there with DS McNeill, making sure Becky Crawford was alright.'

'That was in the other room.'

'Aye.' Bain held his gaze. 'But I saw it all happen through the window. Exactly like they said. Knifey-knifey, thwacky baton, punchy, elbow-y, slippy slippy. Cullen looked like a bit of a clown as he fell, but Falconer pushed him. And I thought the Sundance Kid here was dead. Then he slipped as he was away to stab Hunter.'

Shepherd stared at his shoes, his fist clenching around his umbrella. He shifted his gaze between them. 'I don't believe any of you, but it's not like I've got a choice. This isn't for me to get to the bottom of. It's a Professional Standards case. DI Bain, as commanding officer here, it's going to be on you to defend your actions.'

Bain shrugged. 'Nothing to defend, Luke.'

Shepherd narrowed his eyes at him, then glared at Cullen, giving him a full blast of the ire reserved for Bain.

Bain jerked into action and stepped over to stand near Cullen. 'Cullen, are you fit to serve?'

'Slight bruising, but paramedic let me go. So, aye.'

'Okay, well I want you to get the docs to check you out. While you're waiting, can you and DC Gordon guard Kenny Falconer's ward? I don't want him getting out or anyone getting in until myself or DS Shepherd here turn up. Okay?'

'Sure thing, sir.'

A finger almost touched Cullen's nose. 'Just keep an eye on Kenny while he's treated, okay?' Bain waited for a nod then focused on Hunter. 'Meanwhile, Craig, I'm not letting you out of my sight. You and me are going to interview Becky Crawford.' He leaned in to whisper. 'Just try not to kill anyone else, aye?'

30

Bain

Not sure if I should've put up more of a fight back there in the pissing rain, but sometimes you've got to keep your powder dry. Unlike my clothes. Christ, it stinks of wet dog in here, probably from laughing boy Hunter.

Did I do the right thing? Told a porkie pie the size of Alaska and for what? To protect those two fannies. Cullen and Hunter

Of course I didn't see anything, I was inside and helping that wee Elvis fud tuck into Snickers. Starving this morning. No haggis roll, just a can of WakeyWakey and tearing into that daft sod Ricky, then over here. Stomach's rumbling something rotten — told Elvis those bars were out of date. No doubt repeat on me all day.

Still. Here we are, fresh from saving the damsel in distress. That wee lassie. Becky Crawford. Fringe so low it shouldn't be possible to see through it. Not that she's looking at us. Her chair's pushed back and she's focused on the floor, like she dropped her keys there.

Glad Hunter is here, because I'm not exactly paying attention.

Who does that fanny Shepherd think he is? Telling me what to do? Suppose it's his boss's case and the pair of them dropped a sufficiently big bollock that it required me and Butch to come on and pick it up.

Christ, I love that nickname. That's got legs, I tell you.

'Becky.' Hunter leans forward, not that she's looking at him. 'You want to talk to me. Really, you do.'

She shakes her head. No lawyer, but she's been schooled by someone, and someone good.

'See, Becky, you were supposed to be in court to testify. A lot of people would understand why it's hard to do that. Facing the man who raped you. Must be close to impossible. But you'd been really strong, Becky. You'd assured us you would stand up there and tell the truth. You knew it wasn't just for yourself, but for the other victims of your attacker.'

More head shaking.

Hunter runs a chunky finger down the length of the dressing on his arm. 'When we caught Kenny, I got my arm sliced open.' He's omitting the fact that he did that by clambering through a broken window, not by Falconer's fair hand, but hey ho. I saw the wound and it looked ripe. Amazing what they can do, eh? 'Thing I don't get, Becky, is why run to Kenny?'

She looks up at him now, eyes wide.

'Why go to *him*, Becky?'

'He owns the shop where I work.'

'Right. Sure. You work in Boab's Books?'

'Morning shift, aye.' She nibbles at her lips. 'Got a pub job at night. Had to get someone to cover my shift yesterday cos I was in court.'

'Kenny use that place for money laundering?'

'What? No!'

'Sure about that?'

'Sure I'm sure. Why would you think that?'

'Stands to reason. Selling second-hand books is a cash business. Makes it very easy for people like Kenny to run their ill-gotten gains through the till. Lets them turn very dirty money into nice clean cash.'

She shrugs and maybe the lassie actually doesn't have a scoobie about money laundering. 'It's just a bookshop.'

'Aye. Suspect if we look into the books of the place, it'll—'

'The books of a bookshop?'

'You know what I mean! The accounts. The books. Not the novels. I suspect it's a very lucrative business. Probably sell more than Waterstones on George Street.'

'Look, I don't know anything about that.' And it's a long shot. Another thing we could've added to the pile of charges against Kenny Falconer. Keep that wee bastard locked up as long as we can.

'But you will be able to answer questions on the boo — accounts, right? I mean, if you work there every morning then you'll put a lot of cash through the till.'

Another shrug. 'Whatever.'

And Hunter was doing so well, wasn't he? Almost had me believing in him! Christ.

Sod it.

I lean forward, clunking my elbows hard off the table. Makes her look over at us. Makes me wince. That was a bit too hard, likes. 'Why didn't you show up for court, Becky?'

'Couldn't do it.'

'Right. Because Alexander Drake threatened you, right?'

'He didn't.'

'No, I bet. But somebody did. Eh?'

'No.'

'Come on, Becky. You were *raped*. That must've been horrific. Then to have the bravery to speak to my colleagues, to go through all the tests and the statements. And to agree to stand up in court and testify. Takes a lot of guts. And you had it. But you didn't show up. Meaning someone got to you, eh?'

But she's keeping shtum. Clever girl. See what I mean about whoever's schooling her being good?

'Thing is, when you didn't show, they brought me in to find you. Okay? I'm not like a bounty hunter or anything, but I do my job pretty well. Trouble is, Mr Drake had a second passport. When he walked out of court on bail, he buggered off to Newcastle. Got on a flight to South America via Amsterdam. He's escaped. He won't face justice for what he did to you.'

The tension in her shoulders slipped away.

'Becky, he's in Argentina. No extradition. Clever guy. All he had to do was get his mates to put the fear of death into you, then wait for you to not show up. And he could bugger off on bail. But maybe they kidnapped you?'

She won't look at us.

'A case like that, they can be hard when it's just he said, she said. But we know Drake raped you, right? It wasn't just a case of your word against his. We had your statement backed up by forensics. Juries love forensics. It's science. It's facts. It's truth. But we needed both that lovely evidence and your testimony. Drake was on trial, going down for five years, plus whatever else we can get to stick to him. And anything from whatever he spills on the drugs case we've got against him. But your absence threw it all into chaos. Let him escape the country. Escape justice.'

Still nothing from her. Christ, this is like interviewing a rock.

Wait. Her fingers are twitching.

There we go.

'Thing is, Becky, you were in Kenny's building, weren't you? Keep coming back to it, but what were you doing there?'

Becky looks up, first at me, then at Hunter, then back at me. She's blinking, hard, then fast, those eyelashes like wee butterflies. Tears flood her cheeks, dragging her stale mascara down her face.

'Why, Becky? Why did you go there? Did he take you there?'

'I didn't go there by choice.' She digs the heels of her palms into her eye sockets. 'I was on the phone to DS Shepherd. On my way to the bus stop. Had to take two buses to get to court. But they got me.'

'Who did?'

'Kenny and this... This arsehole who works for him. Doug or Dean or Davie or something. They picked me up on the street. I had no choice. Then they drove me to that place. Kept me there overnight.' She swallows hard. 'All they gave me to eat were these dodgy Snickers bars.'

Christ. 'Dodgy, how?'

She shrugs. 'But when I said I was hungry, Kenny put the box next to me. And I was so hungry.'

'Becky, why are they dodgy?'

'I don't know. They're fakes from South America, I think. The milk in them is dodgy.'

'Dodgy how?'

'Laced with drugs.'

Oh, bloody hell. That's another lost afternoon to the toilet.

'Supposed to be a new drug on the street but it never took off.'

Christ's sake. I ate one! I'll be high as a kite!

She hauls her hair back, pulling the bangs from out of her eyes. 'You want the truth? Kenny... He...' She swallows hard, then looks around the room at a collection of blokes. 'He sexually assaulted me.'

I sit back in my seat and fold my arms. Well, well, well. Didn't expect that. 'Kenny? But we—'

'I know what you're going to say.' She nods, lips pursed together. 'I was at work in the shop, right? Kenny came in, shut the door and took me upstairs.'

And that matches the tale she'd told us. Trouble is, the names had been changed to protect the guilty. 'Becky, we did a rape kit on you. The DNA matched Drake's.'

She shrugs.

'Becky, we've got *evidence* against Drake. His semen. His blood. *He* raped you. You were going to testify against him. Not Kenny.'

'Kenny raped me too.' She grits her teeth so hard it looks like her jaw might break. 'After Kenny raped me. Wore a condom. He got me to have a shower. Then he made Drake do it too.'

'Made him?'

'At knifepoint.'

'He raped you when Kenny had a knife to his neck?'

'No, but the threat was there. And that's why all the evidence pointed to Sandy.'

Christ. What a filthy little degenerate. I mean...

Hunter doesn't seem to be buying this, mind. 'Why do you still work for him?'

'It's tough. Kenny pays me a lot of money. Mostly to keep quiet. And some of it is... My habit.'

'Drugs?'

She looks away. 'Right.'

Christ, the poor lassie. All this hassle she's got herself into. Never ends up right for them, does it?

'Becky.' Hunter waits for her to look at him. 'I need you to be honest. One last time. Did it happen like that?'

She nods.

'In that case, you were raped by two men. One is in Argentina and we can't get to him, but the other, Kenny

Falconer, he's in hospital. Just up the road. We've got him, Becky. We can't prosecute him for this crime, but there are others he's behind. We would like you to give us a statement and for you to stand up in court and testify against him. Then he'll go to prison. He won't be able to get at you. And your drug problem, we can put you into the best programmes for that. Okay?'

She isn't looking at him.

'Becky, when women like you end up in difficult situations like this, it's very often fatal. Someone like Kenny Falconer or the man who comes after him, they have a habit of killing people like you. This is your chance to strike back against them.'

She's shaking her head.

'Becky, I spoke to your parents this morning. They love you. They're hurt by what happened to you. Between you and them. I can get them in here. I can—'

'Are you trying to use that against me? To get me to—?'

'No. I'll get them in here, whatever happens. You deserve to be reunited with them.'

She shuts her eyes. 'Okay.'

'Okay?'

'Okay, I'll testify.'

'Thank you, Becky.'

31

Cullen

'Sure you're okay, big man?' Elvis was sitting the other side of the door, eyes wide.

Cullen sat back and stared at the ceiling tiles. 'I'm fine.'

And he wasn't. Not in the slightest. It felt like he'd fallen off a roof onto a police car.

All that metal fighting back against him, pushing against him. And the state of the thing after he'd got off, the roof all crumpled in.

And Kenny Falconer had "fallen" onto him, smashing his weight against Cullen's hip. A skinny wee sod, maybe, but gravity had a habit of turning skinny wee sods into fast-moving heavy objects. And getting pinned between Falconer and the car, double ouch.

Still, they had Falconer in custody. While the doctor was seeing to him, Cullen and Elvis were outside, trapping him in there. The room's windows couldn't open. Kenny Falconer was down.

'Sure you're fine?' Elvis was shaking his head. 'Because you—'

The door swished open and Dr Yule stepped out. She sighed at the sight of Cullen, then gave them both a smile. 'Constable, I need a word.'

Cullen and Elvis were both on their feet.

'Not you, Paul.' Helen was smiling at Elvis. 'Just Scott.'

'Oh, but we're—'

'Guarding Mr Falconer, yes. I get it. Your job is to sit there and guard, which is usually a one-man task. I've been told to give DC Cullen a once-over. Assuming he passes fit, you can both do it.' She smiled again then crossed the corridor into an office, holding the door open for Cullen.

Cullen eased up to his feet, but it felt like he was carrying three sacks of coal around his neck. 'Just stay here, Paul. Don't leave without me.'

'Will do.' Elvis was already staring at his phone.

Cullen crossed the corridor, yawning, and entered the office.

Helen shut the door behind him and took her glasses off, resting them on a desk. Then she lurched forward and latched her mouth onto his, kissing so deep. And her hands crawled all over his body, up his back and into his trousers.

Pain flashed up his hip, but he ignored it, grabbing hold of her buttocks and biting her bottom lip.

She pushed against the door with a thud, pinning his torso.

Cullen yelped.

She stepped back, wiping her mouth. 'Are you okay?'

'Not really. I fell from a roof onto a car, then laughing boy over there landed on me.'

'Jesus, Scott!'

'I saw a paramedic, who okayed it.'

'You fell onto a car?'

'Aye, I'm okay.' But Cullen was frowning. 'What was that chat about giving me a once-over?'

'Well, I just needed an excuse to get you alone. I'm pretty horny.'

'So, I take it we're an item, then?'

She put her glasses back on and gazed at him through the thick lenses. 'Aye, but seriously. You should probably have an X-ray.'

'I'm fine.'

'No, yelping like my wee Scottie dog isn't fine.'

Cullen leaned towards her and gave her a kiss, soft and tender this time. 'Okay, so maybe I'm not so fine, but I'm not in a bad place.'

'Just take care of yourself, Scott, that's all I ask.'

'Aye, I know. Nature of the beast.' He took her hand and clenched it tight. 'How about catching up when I'm back from Christmas?'

She fixed him with a hard stare. 'You're going away?'

'Three weeks, aye. Got a few things on at home. I'll come back for a couple of days around Christmas and we can get—'

'You live in Angus, right?'

'Dalhousie, aye. Wee shithole on the coast between Arbroath and Montrose.'

'Well, I'm seeing my sister in Perth. Perhaps we can—'

'Sure.' Cullen shrugged. 'I like Perth.'

'But you'd rather meet in Edinburgh?'

'Well, meeting in Perth means we get to know each other, right? Without the pressure of sex.'

'The pressure of sex?'

'You know what I mean, Helen. Going on a date. It gives you time to grow to despise how much I sigh or my politics.'

'You're not a Tory, are you?'

'Christ, no. Why?'

'Well, you're a cop.'

'And you're a doctor. Goes with both territories.'

'Mm, true.' She was frowning hard. 'Okay. It's a date.' She took off her glasses again and kissed him hard, her teeth bumping against his, her fingers digging into his cheeks, then broke off with a gasp. 'Thank you for not asking me about seeing Kenny Falconer.'

Cullen arched an eyebrow. 'How is he?'

'Well, he's got cracked ribs.'

'Prognosis?'

'A couple of weeks and he'll be right as rain.'

'So, on remand in the hospital over Christmas?'

'Right enough.'

Something clattered in the corridor. Something hard thumped into the door. Someone screamed and something else clattered.

Cullen twisted the handle and pulled the door open.

A hospital cart was lying arse over tit, all the equipment scattered across the tiles. Elvis was leaning against Falconer's door, with a pair of scissors sticking out of his thigh, but was just staring into space like he'd eaten a very strong hash cake in Amsterdam.

And Kenny Falconer stood over him, brandishing a scalpel.

Cullen reached into his jacket for his baton. He snapped it to extend it and as he stepped through his swing, Falconer slashed out with the knife, missing

Cullen by millimetres. The baton hit the wall and the shockwave ran up Cullen's arm like a hammer blow.

Helen screamed out. Clutched her eye.

Falconer smashed Cullen's kneecap with his bare foot, then shot along the corridor, away from the cart.

Cullen stood there, unable to move. Unable to choose.

Stop Falconer escaping.

Or stay with Helen, hoping security caught the bastard.

Cullen tugged the emergency cord and knelt next to her, trying to prise her blood-soaked fingers away from her skull. 'Are you okay?'

'No!' Her eyebrow was bisected by a deep wound that ran down into her eye socket and across the closed lid.

No contest.

32

Hunter

Hunter didn't want to look at his arm. Any time he moved it, the bandages dug into the hairs and gave a different flavour of burn, like someone had taken a blowtorch to it.

Which hauled him back to a hotter time. Night, the sound of distant gunfire. The smell of burning meat.

He tried to centre himself on the here and now.

The swoosh of the cleaning machine further down the corridor.

'Thanks for waiting with me.'

'It's what mates are for.' Chantal Jain was leaning forward, thumbs hammering off the keys of her mobile. 'Had one before?'

'An HIV test?' He winced. 'A couple of times.'

She smirked at him. 'Bad boy.'

'Hardly.' Hunter looked away from her. 'Once when I was back in Iraq. Exploding body parts have a surprisingly high probability of getting into your mouth, especially when you're shocked and it's hanging wide. And I had an open wound from a knife fight with a warlord.'

'Gross.' She was giving him some wild side eye. 'And also, a knife fight with a warlord?'

'Long, long story. I'm not very good with knives.' Hunter winced. 'Unlike Kenny Falconer.'

She held his gaze for a really long time. Felt like weeks. 'Heard you hurled him off the side of the building.'

'That's bollocks.'

'Thought so. Still, people talk. Especially cops.'

'It was slippery as hell up there. Absolutely pissing down.' Hunter's trousers were slicked to his thighs and his shoes made him feel like he was paddling on the beach at Porty. 'Christ, at least we've got Becky to testify.'

'Aye, good work on that score.' Jain smiled. 'We'll prosecute Kenny for this. Murders, drug deals, rapes. All of it.' Her phone chimed, then rang way louder than it should be in a hospital. She checked the display. 'Got to take this.' She walked off, looking back at him with a frown, mouthing, 'You okay?'

Hunter raised his thumb. And got a fresh burn of pain.

She answered the phone. 'Hi, sir.' Then disappeared around a corner.

Hunter stood up and peered through the window into the ward.

Happy Jack was still sitting by a bed, head in his hands. The news about his wife's death was hitting him way harder than Hunter expected.

She had a name. Marie Richardson. Ran away from Elgin and an abusive relationship. Fell in with a bad crowd in Glasgow, then moved through to Edinburgh where she found an even worse one. Two years living with junkies in a shooting gallery in Muirhouse, and she found salvation in Happy Jack. And free heroin. The free heroin that cost her life.

Hunter should get in there, question him. See if any of Jonathan Braithwaite was coming out to play today. And maybe get something they could use against Falconer.

But that was for another day.

Hunter sat back on his chair and rested his sore arm in his hand.

Bloody mess. This case. His life. All of it.

Kenny Falconer. At least they had him.

So why was he standing at the end of the corridor, in a gown, glowering at Hunter.

'Stop!' Hunter launched to his feet and clattered after him.

But Falconer was quick, shooting off back the way he'd come.

Hunter followed, but lost him around the first corner. Trouble with this place was it all looked the same. Bleached-white corridors, rooms all leading off. Falconer could be in any of them.

Or he could be up ahead.

Just great.

Weren't Elvis and Cullen supposed to be looking after him?

Hunter ran along the corridor and turned another corner, and almost smacked into a cleaning machine. He waved a hand at the operator, getting him to lift his headphones off but he didn't stop. 'Have you see anyone run this way?'

A frown crossed the jutting forehead. 'Think so.'

'Where?'

The operator thumbed behind him.

'Thanks.' Hunter raced off, passing four closed doors and he swung around another corner. 'Holy shit.'

Elvis lay against a door, a pool of thick blood leeching out of his thigh. He was grinning at the pair of scissors jabbed into his leg, stoned out of his skull. On God knows what.

Shite, those Snickers bars. The daft sod had been eating them.

Opposite, Cullen lifted Dr Yule up in his arms. 'Craig, I need your help!'

Hunter had no choice. He'd lost Falconer.

Again.

33

Bain

One job.

These arseholes had one job.

Christ on a bike.

Cullen is sitting in front of the CCTV machine, knees up to his oxters. Not that he's looking at us, instead rocking the footage back and forward, switching between all the views available.

Tell you, the stuff at the CCTV station in the Royal Mile is decades behind this stuff. Instead of these arseholes stopping Kenny bloody Falconer escaping from the hospital, we can just watch him stabbing Elvis in the thigh with a pair of bloody scissors, then cutting that doctor bird in the eye with a scalpel, then escaping from the hospital. In high-resolution, Techni-bloody-color.

Christ.

I rest a hand on Cullen's shoulder. 'What were you doing when this happened?'

Cullen taps the screen, at the door opposite Elvis. An office, maybe. 'I was in there, discussing Kenny Falconer's prognosis with Dr Yule.'

Up to his nuts in her, more like. Dirty wee shagger.

'And what did she say?'

'Said it was good, could interview him soon.' Cullen squints at the screen. He's good. Used to lying to bosses, isn't he? Could use a lad like this on my team. 'Not as good a prognosis as mine, but then he bounced off me and fell onto the tarmac.'

'Pair of arseholes.'

Cullen looks around at us, eyebrow raised. 'Thanks for backing up our story.'

'What, with Shepherd?'

'Aye.'

'Well, you owe me now.' It's a whisper.

Cullen nods, but he's definitely heard us. Still, he's focusing on the screen. 'That's interesting.'

And he's right. Kenny waltzes out the front of the hospital in a business suit, fancy specs dazzling the camera. Stops a cab and gets in.

'I'll have to trace this, sir. And we should see whose suit he stole.'

'Damn right.'

Cullen gets out his phone and walks away from us, out into the corridor. Can see him through the wired glass.

Leaving me scratching my balls in there. I reach over to the big jog wheel doodah so I can have a little fiddle with the footage but all I get is the screen going blank.

Useless piece of shite!

The door swings open and Cullen steps back in.

'Can you fix this?'

'Fix it yourself.' It's not Cullen, but Hunter, giving us the kind of glower that could melt a tank.

And he's with Elvis, who seems to be in orbit around Saturn, his eyes almost all pupil.

Those Snickers bars. Don't seem to be melting yours truly in the same way, mind.

'All that work getting her to agree to testify, it's not much use if we've lost Falconer, is it?' Hunter stands up tall, almost a foot above us. 'And the doctors told me I've got to take Paul here home. His leg's fine, the scissors somehow managed to miss veins and arteries. But those Snickers bars he was eating were loaded with cannabis resin.'

Shite.

A burp escapes my gut. 'How many did he eat?'

'Sixteen.'

'*Sixteen*?' Christ, well that would explain it. I only had one. 'He going to be okay?'

'Docs have given him something for it. Sedative or an upper or something. Got to take him home, get him to bed. Let him sleep it all off.'

'Well, what's keeping you?'

Hunter doesn't seem to want to get out of here. 'How's it going with finding Falconer?'

I nod over at the door. 'Sundance is checking on something for me.'

'Sundance?'

I smirk, just in time for Cullen to waltz back through.

'That's a no-go on the car.' He pockets his phone. 'ANPR lost it coming off the bypass near Wester Hailes.'

Hunter frowns at him. 'Where Kenny lives. He'll have gone to ground. We won't find him.'

'Great.' I could punch something or someone, but either of these fannies would probably just break. 'So Kenny Falconer's missing. Christ. I need all hands to the pumps, lads. Hunter, you seem to know the boy, so I want you taking lead in Treasure Island.'

'Treasure Island?'

Christ, what do they teach laddies at Tulliallan. 'Wester bloody Hailes!'

'Sir.' Hunter gives us a nice big nod. The kind that shows a healthy amount of respect for authority. 'On it. Oh, and I just wanted to say that I checked in on Dr Yule, but she's still in surgery.'

'But?'

'But that's it. And if you want me working, someone needs to get Elvis home.'

'Fine, if you could speak to Butch, I'd appreciate it.'

'Butch?'

Can't hide my smirk, can I? 'DS McNeill.'

'Will do.' Hunter heads for the door.

Cullen's blocking his way. 'Wondered if you needed a hand?'

Hunter laughs in his face. 'Find another mate.' He shakes his head and barges through him and the door.

Cullen stands there, frowning at him like he's just lost a lover. Maybe he has. You get anything in the police these days, eh?

I get in front of him. 'You couldn't take Elvis, could you?'

Cullen scratches his neck. 'Trouble is, I'm signed off.'

'Sick?'

'Aye. Took a header off the roof, didn't I?'

'You told me you were cleared.'

'Well, thing is. Dr Yule was inspecting my injuries. Kenny landed on me and it hurts like hell.'

'Man up, Sundance.'

He winces at the name. 'Sir, I'm not even on duty today.'

'You should know that Saturdays aren't sacrosanct in CID. And I found you kipping under your desk, you drunken idiot.'

'It's not that, sir, I—'

'Christmas party last night. I get it. Blackout. Hungover. Sleepy time.'

'No, I'm catching a train back home. It's a mate's wedding tomorrow.'

'Oh, right. Can we speak on Monday?'

'Well, I'm finished up for Christmas now until January. Three weeks off.'

'Christ. How the hell have you swung that?'

'All that sick leave I was talking about? The annual leave stacks up if you don't take it and I can't roll it forward.'

Christ, Shepherd is a soft bastard.

'The way you stayed with the doc, the way you protected her, the way you tracked Falconer down. That's impressive work.'

'Cheers, sir.' But he's looking impatient and ready to bugger off. 'I was going to check in on Dr Yule.'

I raise a hand. 'By all means.'

34

Cullen

A few hours ago, Cullen had been kissed to within an inch of his life in this room. He'd never been kissed like that. Not by anyone. Maybe he'd met his match.

Now, he was sitting with Dr Gupta, freaking out about what he might have lost. 'Will she be okay?'

Gupta nodded his head, spreading out his double chin into at least another couple. 'She's going to be fine, aye.' His west coast accent was sharp like broken glass.

Cullen let the held breath escape his lips. 'Thank Christ for that.'

'Nothing to do with any gods or demigods, I'm afraid. All down to you.'

'Hardly.'

'If you'd chased after her attacker, Helen would've lost the eye. As it is, she's got a cut. A deep abrasion, mind, but only a cut. And her eye will be okay. '

'Seriously?'

'Totally fine. We're transferring her to the eye pavilion in the next ten minutes where she will get the best care. Her only risk is infection. Trust me.'

'Mind if I speak to her?'

'That will be tricky. Dr Yule is on some severely strong painkillers.'

'But she's awake?'

'Aye.'

'Please, can—'

'Go on. But be quick.'

'Will do.' Cullen opened the door and stepped into the room.

Helen lay on the bed, the blankets up to her chin. Half her face was covered by a thick gauze. Hard to see anything. Her free eye settled on Cullen, then looked away.

A nurse stood there, hands on hips. Emma? Erica? Either way, it was the one who Cullen had a terrible date with. No doubt spreading more lies about him.

Her name badge read Anna.

Christ.

'I'll leave you to it.' Nurse Anna gave Cullen the

frostiest look as she passed. 'Five minutes and the porter's taking her to the ambulance.'

'The eye pavilion isn't here?'

'No, Scott. They left it over by the old hospital.' Anna shook her head and left the room.

Helen wouldn't make eye contact with him.

'How are you feeling?'

'I'm finding it tough not standing by the side of the bed with a clipboard. And it's tougher being the one in the bed.'

'Understand that. Like when some wee ned nicked my phone a couple of years ago and I wasn't a cop any more, just another pissed punter with a nicked mobile.'

'Right. It's a bit more serious than that.'

'I loved that phone.'

'*Scott.*'

Cullen huffed down into the visitor's chair, trying to grin away the failed humour. 'Dr Gupta said your eye will be okay.'

'I'm less sure of that than he is.' She patted the bandage. 'But I'll have a hell of a scar.'

Cullen smiled at that, but it soon frosted over. 'Helen, I keep replaying what happened. I wish there was some way I could've stopped it. If he'd slashed me instead of you.'

'But this is what happened, Scott.'

'But I got you involved in it.'

'What?' She sat up in her bed. 'No, you didn't. I'm a doctor in A&E, Scott. My job is to literally be here. Accepting danger is as much part of my job as it is yours.'

Cullen rubbed at the back of his neck. 'It was my job to secure Falconer, but I didn't.'

'No, because you were kissing me in my office.'

'And what a kiss.' Cullen raised his eyebrows. 'I loved it.'

'Thank you for staying with me. Dave Gupta said if you'd not carried me into the ward, I could've lost the eye. Or caught an infection.'

'I really wish it hadn't happened.'

'But it did, Scott.' She looked at him, her gaze piercing him. 'When's your train?'

'Half six.'

She frowned at the wall. 'That was an hour ago?'

'I missed it. Going to drive up later. I needed to see you, Helen.'

She let out a deep breath. 'Scott, I don't think you and me is a good idea.'

'What? Why not?'

'I just don't.'

'Is it the nurses here?'

'Anna was talking about you. They all do. The thing is, I've got trust issues. Maybe that's being harsh, but you try going out with three different men who were shagging other women behind your back and see how you feel.'

'I'm sorry to hear that.'

'Scott, I just can't handle going out with you. Not with the way you are. Not with the way I am. When I pushed you against the door? Aye, you're a great kisser, but we both need to work on being better human beings.'

'Can we try it together?'

'I don't think so, Scott.'

Cullen sat there. He could fight. He could charm. He could do any number of things. But maybe admitting defeat, letting her win, maybe that was the right thing to do here. Respect her.

He got to his feet. 'I'm glad you're okay, Helen.'

'No hard feelings?'

'None.' Cullen smiled at her. 'I'll work on being a better person. And if you change your mind, you've got my phone number.'

She smiled and nodded.

Cullen left her to it and wiped the tear from his cheek.

'You crying there, Sundance?'

Cullen swivelled around and caught Bain's glare. 'Dr Yule's going to be fine.'

'Aye, so I gather.' Bain wandered over, hands in pockets. 'Been wondering if this is the right thing, but sod it. Aye, of course it is. Earlier, when we were driving, what you were saying about your tenure? Well, there's an opening in my team. Full DC role, tenured for five years, working for Sharon McNeill.' He grinned wide. 'Bugger me, I absolutely love Butch as a nickname. Have to call you Sundance, of course.'

Cullen tried to laugh it off. Best practise for a bully; don't give them the satisfaction.

'And I'd love to keep Butch and Sundance together as a team. While you have lots to learn, I think you have bags of potential. And you'll have an ADC working for you too, like you are to that clown Hunter. It'll give you a chance to develop management skills. Got this wee bastard starting, rough diamond who needs polishing.'

Cullen let the breath escape his lips, nice and slow. All the things he'd asked for, given to him on a plate. 'But I let Kenny Falconer go.'

'You're one of those types, eh?' Bain shook his head. 'No, Sundance. Falconer stabbed Elvis with scissors, then knifed a doctor in the eye. You saved her. I can do with that kind of hero on my team.'

'I'll need to think about it.'

'Well, you've got the job if you want it. But I need the answer now.'

Cullen opened his eyes wide. 'That's the interview?'

'Aye. It's how I roll. Seen how you work, and you seem to be a match for the team. You want it? You got it.'

Cullen nodded as fast and hard as he could. Like saving Helen's eye, it wasn't really a choice. 'I do.'

'See you in the New Year down in Leith Walk, Sundance.' Bain clamped a fist around his arm. 'Maybe one day we'll catch Kenny Falconer.'

35

Shepherd

Ten years later

Shepherd wound around yet another corner. One of those roads that couldn't decide which direction it wanted to go in, so took all of them. And giant hills on both sides blocked any view of any landmarks. And the hills all looked the same. No trees, of course, this was the Highlands. Just sheep as far as the eye could see.

He kept an eye on the battery meter, hoping the

range on his Tesla would get him there. Seemed okay, but it could dip.

The giant screen lit up as the podcast changed episode.

'Welcome to the Secret Rozzer podcast.' The voice was all distorted and mangled. 'Coming up in this week's episode, a story about young Sundance waking up under his desk after a work night out. Poor lamb had blacked out. But first, a word from our sponsors.'

Shepherd drove on, but he really couldn't figure out why they'd put so much of this in the public domain. If you knew it was Cullen they were talking about, you knew he'd been getting no end of grief from his bosses. But it made him wonder what else they had on him.

And it made him relieved that he hadn't confronted Cullen and Hunter last week. McKeown's intervention led him down a nice path. Some old faces, some new ones too. But he'd gained so much.

Somehow Cullen had made DI and Shepherd couldn't fathom why. Maybe there were successful stories he hadn't heard in his time working around Scotland, away from Edinburgh. Maybe Cullen just knew the right people.

Wait, there was the wind farm, the turbines lazily swatting the thick air around. Next right, but it seemed to take ages to get to anything like it. The car, at least, barely rattled as he took the cattle grid slowly, but Shepherd felt it in his fillings.

A thin path led up between two monstrous hills, the kind you'd see for half the country if they were in the lowlands, but seemed average up here, drowned out by Munros and lesser mountains.

And there it was, nestled between two minor hills. Sundance Acres.

Shepherd pulled in and parked up in one of the three spaces. Not the first Tesla parked there. He grabbed his warrant card and got out to stretch. One thing about driving straight from Edinburgh is it made his whole body ache.

A door rattled open and small feet crunched over pebbles, with larger ones making a bigger dent.

'You found it, then?' Bain stood in a silver-grey Mogwai T-shirt, even though it was two-jumpers-and-a-jacket weather. Hands tucked into his jeans pocket. He looked fit and well, clean-shaven for once. He darted forward and scooped up a hyper-active toddler into his arms. 'Why don't you go and tell your mummy that our guest's here?'

The girl squealed and skittered off.

Bain watched her go back inside. 'Got a super charger if you need it.' He tapped his own car, a Model X. At least twice the price of Shepherd's.

'That'd be fantastic, aye.' Shepherd caught the

nozzle and plugged it in. An hour and he could get going. If they needed that long.

Bain folded his arms across his T-shirt. Didn't seem to be the sort to have even heard of the band. 'Nice interior, though. Bit of an upgrade on mine.' He leaned over to plug in Shepherd's car. 'Got to wonder where a cop gets the money for a Model 3.'

'Want the truth or a lie?'

'Whatever you're most comfortable with, Luke.'

'You must have an inkling.'

'Oh aye, I do. And it's why you've driven all this way. You're not DS Luke Shepherd, are you?'

Shepherd smiled. Christ, Bain had been off the force over a year and he knew the deepest secrets. 'Someone leaking in your boozer?'

'Got it in one. And it's DCI Luke Shepherd, right?'

'Right.'

'Working for Professional Standards and Ethics.'

'That's why I'm here, Brian. Time was, I'd have been investigating you, but now…'

'Now, you're looking into what the hell Scott Cullen and Craig Hunter have been up to.'

'Possibly.'

'Well, you've come to the right place. Thanks to my little investment back in Edinburgh, I've amassed a few massive files on those two.' Bain straightened himself up and rubbed his hands together. 'Let's get started, eh?'

But Shepherd didn't move. He could just get a few minutes' charge into the car, enough to get to Inverness, then find a charger there. Be away from the creepy bastard.

No, he needed to know if Bain was on the level. 'Don't waste any more of my time, Brian. What's your smoking gun?'

'Surprised a man of your means hasn't found it.'

'I gather it's from the Kenny Falconer case?'

'Partly.'

'If I remember, you were the one who stood up for them. Told me that you saw Kenny slip, rather than Hunter throwing him.'

'I backed them up. Trouble was, I backed the wrong horse. That was the beginning of the end for me. I let Cullen onto my team. Kind of like letting a vampire into your house, Luke. Either way, you're getting blood sucked from your neck. Should maybe have been Team Hunter, eh? But those two got pally again, didn't they?'

'Driving up here, to listen what I already knew. I've wasted my time, then.'

'Should've listened when I said "partly", Luke. Got a few angles on those two. Word is that young Yvonne Flockhart is shacked up with Cullen nowadays.'

'That's right. Been a couple of years. Why?'

'Curious thing, the first search Yvonne did that Monday morning she was back at work was for a woman called Carnegie in the Angus area. A teacher. You any idea who that might be?'

Shepherd did, but the worst part was that Bain did now too.

And now Shepherd knew how bad it was going to get for Scott Cullen.

To be concluded in "THE LAST DROP", coming November 2021.

AFTERWORD

This book was originally published as the fifth Cullen and Bain novel, but I've moved it back to the first in the series, as it's the chronologically correct place for it.

I had to delay publishing it for a few months – I was on a track to finishing this whole series by Christmas last year, then a spot of heart arrhythmia and bang, no books for a long time. Anyway, I'm all better now and recovered. And back in this world.

This story has lurked in my brain since the first Craig Hunter book, where I needed to figure out why they were such bitter enemies (on one side, anyway). It also gave me an opportunity to explore why Cullen is the way he is. And hopefully you'll enjoy this as a new reader – this is a precinct series, like Ed McBain's books, though the first few are about Cullen. I plan to write more in the series later on.

Thanks to Allan Guthrie, James Mackay, Colin Scott and Mare Bate for their help with this book. You're all the best!

And you. Hope you enjoy this and the wait for the last one isn't too long.

— Ed

Scottish Borders, 2023

SCOTT CULLEN WILL RETURN

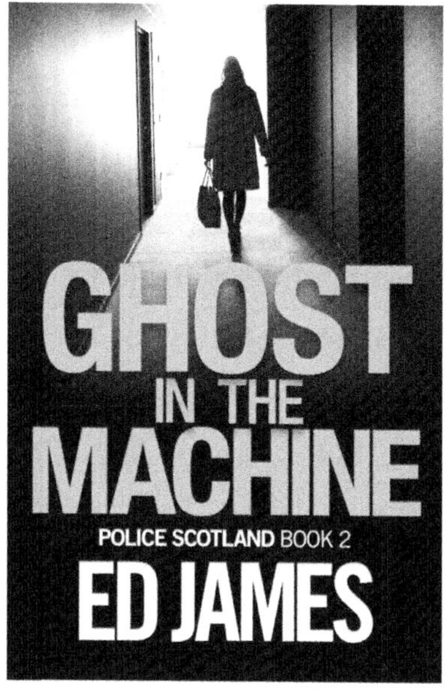

Think you're safe online? Think again.

DC Scott Cullen of Lothian and Borders CID has only been in the job three months. Young, eager to please and desperate to do good. So a missing persons case should be an easy case to solve. Right?

Fresh from a messy divorce, Caroline Adamson's future is finally looking up. Her son seems happy and she's dating again. Trouble is, Cullen can't find Caroline or the man she met on Schoolbook, the latest social network taking Edinburgh by storm.

When Caroline's mutilated body is found, Edinburgh faces the reality of a serial killer hunting young women. The discovery of a second, connected victim leads DI Brian Bain to put Caroline's ex-husband in the frame. Cullen isn't so sure and is determined that the right person faces justice. As things take a personal turn, Cullen must look closer to home for the answer — before it's too late.

Get it now!

If you would like to be kept up to date with new releases from Ed James and access free novellas, please join the Ed James Readers' Club:

http://geni.us/EJmailer

ABOUT THE AUTHOR

Ed James is the author of the bestselling DI Simon Fenchurch novels, Seattle-based FBI thrillers starring Max Carter, and the self-published Detective Scott Cullen series and its Craig Hunter spin-off books.

During his time in IT project management, Ed spent every moment he could writing and has now traded in his weekly commute to London in order to write full-time. He lives in the Scottish Borders with far too many rescued animals.

If you would like to be kept up to date with new releases from Ed James, please join the Ed James Readers Club.

Connect with Ed online:

Amazon Author page

Website

OTHER BOOKS BY ED JAMES

DI ROB MARSHALL

Ed's first new police procedural series in six years, focusing on DI Rob Marshall, a criminal profiler turned detective. London-based, an old case brings him back home to the Scottish Borders and the dark past he fled as a teenager.

1. THE TURNING OF OUR BONES
2. WHERE THE BODIES LIE (May 2023)

Also available is FALSE START, a prequel novella starring DS Rakesh Siyal, is available for **free** to subscribers of Ed's newsletter or on Amazon. Sign up at https://geni.us/EJLCFS

POLICE SCOTLAND

Precinct novels featuring detectives covering Edinburgh and its surrounding counties, and further across Scotland: Scott Cullen, eager to climb the career ladder; Craig Hunter, an ex-squaddie struggling with PTSD; Brian Bain, the centre of his own universe and everyone else's. Previously published as SCOTT CULLEN MYSTERIES, CRAIG HUNTER POLICE THRILLERS and CULLEN & BAIN SERIES.

1. DEAD IN THE WATER
2. GHOST IN THE MACHINE
3. DEVIL IN THE DETAIL
4. FIRE IN THE BLOOD
5. STAB IN THE DARK
6. COPS & ROBBERS
7. LIARS & THIEVES
8. COWBOYS & INDIANS
9. THE MISSING
10. THE HUNTED
11. HEROES & VILLAINS
12. THE BLACK ISLE
13. THE COLD TRUTH
14. THE DEAD END

DS VICKY DODDS

Gritty crime novels set in Dundee and Tayside, featuring a DS juggling being a cop and a single mother.

1. BLOOD & GUTS
2. TOOTH & CLAW
3. FLESH & BLOOD
4. SKIN & BONE
5. GUILT TRIP

DI SIMON FENCHURCH

Set in East London, will Fenchurch ever find what happened to his daughter, missing for the last ten years?

1. THE HOPE THAT KILLS
2. WORTH KILLING FOR
3. WHAT DOESN'T KILL YOU
4. IN FOR THE KILL
5. KILL WITH KINDNESS
6. KILL THE MESSENGER
7. DEAD MAN'S SHOES
8. A HILL TO DIE ON
9. THE LAST THING TO DIE

Other Books

Other crime novels, with Lost Cause set in Scotland and Senseless set in southern England, and the other three set in Seattle, Washington.

- LOST CAUSE
- SENSELESS
- TELL ME LIES
- GONE IN SECONDS
- BEFORE SHE WAKES

GHOST IN THE MACHINE

PROLOGUE

Where was he?

Caroline was still waiting in the bar where they'd arranged to meet. She checked her watch — he was twenty minutes late.

It felt like hours.

She shouldn't have got there half an hour early. She took another sip from her cocktail, staring into the ice.

The music playing on the bar's stereo switched song. She recognised it, something about making him magnificent tonight. She looked over at the barmaid and pointed up at the speakers. 'What's this?'

The barmaid checked a CD case. 'Sleeper. *Atomic*.'

Caroline nodded. 'Thanks.'

Taking a deep breath, she hoped Martin would be magnificent. She rummaged around in her handbag and found her mobile. She opened the Schoolbook app and found her train of messages with him, re-reading the instructions again, just like she had four times on her laptop at home.

No, there it was — meet in the bar of the Jackson Hotel at half seven.

She went into Martin's profile, looking at the baby-blue eyes in the photo, the wide smile, the perfect teeth. Almost too good to be true.

The only messages on his profile were hers — she wondered if she looked like some mad stalker woman.

She scanned around the room again for anyone even vaguely resembling Martin's profile shot. Nobody came close.

Caroline looked over at the barmaid. 'I'm supposed to be meeting someone.' She held up her mobile. 'Has he been in?'

The barmaid inspected Martin's profile for a few seconds before shaking her head and returning the phone. 'Don't recognise him. He's pretty, though.' She wiped the counter with a cloth then pointed at Caroline's mobile. 'Did you meet him on Schoolbook?'

'If you can call it meeting.'

'Happens a lot these days, I suppose.'

'We'd been talking about films on a message board.'

The barmaid moved off to fuss over the coffee machine.

Caroline took another sip and looked back at the message chain stretching back almost two months, the flirtatious subtext getting ever stronger towards the inevitability of their meeting.

She'd not felt that level of connection with anyone for a long time. It felt like he knew everything about her.

Her heart was thudding in her chest. She took another sip to steady her nerves.

The CD switched track again and she started humming along. She made eye contact with the barmaid. 'What's this one?'

The barmaid looked at the box again, her eyes squinting. 'New Order, *Temptation*.'

Caroline frowned, thinking she knew the album. 'What CD it?'

The barmaid held up the box. '*Trainspotting* soundtrack. It's just what was here. Got some decent tunes on it, though.'

'That's my favourite film. It's what we were chatting about on Schoolbook.' Caroline looked down at her glass again and bit her lip. 'Rob bought me that.'

'Who's he?'

'My ex-husband. He's a wanker.'

The barmaid snorted. 'Don't get me started on mine.' She moved off to serve another customer.

Caroline stabbed at her phone, tempted to delete

Rob from her friends list there and then. She should never have accepted his invite in the first place, but she'd been trying to be *friends* for Jack's sake.

She noticed her fists were clenched. She let them go, taking another drink, hoping nobody noticed.

She looked across the bar area, seeing herself in the mirror. She sighed, reflecting on how little had outwardly changed in her — she'd lost weight after having Jack and didn't look much older than her thirty-two years. The divorce had added dark rings around her eyes she just couldn't get rid of.

Her mobile lit up — a text from Amy. '*Jack's just gone to sleep. No more phone calls. A x*'

Caroline swallowed hard, feeling guilty at being out and leaving her son with a friend.

The music changed again. Anger burned through her as she thought of Rob moving on, leaving her with Jack. Not that she resented him it was just—

Caroline put the phone back on the bar.

It buzzed almost immediately — a text from Steve Allen, one of her oldest friends. '*Just on my way to Parkhead, wanted to wish you good luck for tonight. Not that you'll need it.*'

She texted back. '*I don't think I will. You might.*'

She tapped send and the phone rang, an unknown number. Her hands shook as she put it to her ear.

'Caroline, hi, it's Martin.'

His voice was familiar, almost reassuring. She loved Northern Irish accents.

'Hi.' Her voice was a nervous croak. She cleared her throat. 'Hi, Martin.'

'I'm really sorry, but I'm running late. I've just got back from the office, had a last minute meeting thrown at me and I'm only getting ready now. And I left my personal mobile in my hotel room like an idiot.'

Caroline wasn't sure what to make of it. 'That's okay.'

'Tell you what, I'm just about ready now so why don't you come meet me at my room and we'll go on from there?'

'Sure.'

'It's just at the back of the ground floor. Room twenty.'

The phone clicked dead.

Her heart was racing again. She was finally going to meet him. *In person.*

She wondered about meeting him in his room but they'd talked so often on Schoolbook it felt like they'd known each other for years.

She grinned at the barmaid as she got up, leaving the ice at the bottom of her glass. She walked through reception, a brass plate on the wall indicating room 20 was along a wood-panelled corridor.

When she got there, the door was ajar.

She called into the room. No answer.

She frowned and looked back along the corridor, her heart racing.

She took a deep breath and knocked on the door. It opened further.

'Come in.'

She entered.

The door slammed behind her. A hand clasped over her mouth. 'Hello, Caroline.'

As she twisted around, she saw his face. Her eyes bulged.

A rope bit into her neck.

A fist slammed into her skull.

GHOST IN THE MACHINE is out now. You can get a copy at Amazon.

If you would like to be kept up to date with new releases from Ed James, please join the Ed James Readers Club.

Printed in Great Britain
by Amazon